MOUNTAIN OF THE AMERICAN DRAGON

JON SHANNON

NORTH STAR PUBLISHING

ABOUT THIS SERIES

Every generation inherits its own kind of magic. In *The Wilder Chronicles*, that magic belongs to Wilder Blackwood and his dog Bo, a dragon in disguise. Together they travel through Maine and beyond, facing forgotten gods, rogue cryptids, restless spirits, and the quiet mysteries that connect us all.

Each book stands alone but weaves into a larger story about destiny, friendship, and the return of the old world into the new.

Magic is real, just not in the way the stories have told you.

ALSO BY JON SHANNON

Books in this series:

Treasure of the American Dragon

Mountain of the American Dragon

Other books by the author:

The Longest Summer

Collections that include the author's work:

Midnight Garden: Where Dark Tales Grow

(Midnight Anthology Series Book 2)

Midnight Oil: Stories to Fuel Your Nightmares

(Midnight Anthology Series Book 3)

www.jonshannonbooks.com

Copyright © 2025 by Jon Shannon

No portion of this book may be reproduced in any form without written permission from the publisher or author, except as permitted by U.S. copyright law.

For Zach and Spencer.
Thank you for listening to your dad's silly
stories for so many years.

You've been my favorite audience from the start.

A Note from the Author

This story is a work of fiction inspired by the landscapes and legends of Maine.

References to Pamola, the Mikumwess, and other beings of Wabanaki tradition are used here with great respect for the enduring cultural heritage of the Wabanaki peoples. These myths and names belong to living communities whose traditions continue today. Any interpretations or reimaginings in this book are entirely my own and are not intended to represent their sacred stories.

I offer this tale in admiration of their enduring connection to the mountain and its mysteries.

Please seek out Wabanaki artists and historians, and treat their tales with respect as living culture.

CONTENTS

"Pamola is always angry with those who climb to the summit of Katahdin."

Henry David Thoreau

CHAPTER ONE

LOST ON A MOUNTAIN

The Klondike, a remote area northwest of Mt Katahdin, Maine

"Run! They're right behind us!"

Our feet pounded through a dense blanket of pine needles and twigs slick with damp across the forest floor, every step a reminder why i never did track in high school. Moments like this made me thankful for my Timberland boots, even though they're about as good for sprinting as flip-flops in a swamp. Stunted spruce trees blocked every direction, jammed so closely together they may as well have been welded shut. There was no room for Bo to stretch his wings and transform into a dragon. Whatever was chasing us now had friends. The forest shook as massive "things" smashed through the trees from three different directions, herding us forward like cattle. We had no choice but to keep moving in that single open direction. I didn't want the big, ugly mystery creatures to catch up with us.

The forest floor breathed out the stink of rot and wet decay, a compost heap mixed with pine sap, like the woods were running their own all-you-can-eat buffet for rot. Every breath burned in my lungs, every stride jolted through my knees. The forest was alive with noise. Branches snapping, trunks groaning, deep-throated howls echoing between the trees. Pizza and Netflix at home would be way better than running through the woods trying to save the world. I didn't dare look back, because I already knew the sight would freeze me in place.

"This is exactly how every horror movie starts," Bo said, sprinting a few steps ahead. "Spoiler alert: we're the idiots who go into the woods anyway."

"Comforting! That really helps my anxiety right now," I hollered as I stumbled over downed branches.

"That's what sidekicks are for."

A branch cracked somewhere ahead. I froze, debating if I should keep going in the same direction.

"What was that?" I whispered.

"Could be a squirrel. Could be our doom. Want to flip a coin?" Bo said.

"That's not how reassurance works."

Bo is my French bulldog—or at least, that's what most people see. In reality, he's an ancient dragon, over 800 years old. He's been crashing in my third floor apartment for the last few months. In that short time, we've had more than our share of weird, wild, and terrifying adventures. This time, we're about to get eaten, destroyed, or stomped on by whatever is chasing us through the dark northeastern woods of Baxter State Park in Maine. Some people come here to camp or hike in the pristine beauty of the Maine woods. We came here to find the Thunderbirds that have returned and are killing random hikers. Five people disappeared last summer, and we're the only ones who know the actual reason why.

I thought about those hikers now—faces I'd only seen on missing posters tacked up on telephone poles and in gas stations, smiles frozen in yearbook photos. Somewhere out there were families still waiting for answers. I couldn't fail the way the mountain had failed them.

My head smacked into a low-hanging spruce branch I couldn't see in the post-twilight darkness. Stumbling from the aftereffect of essentially being on the baseball end of a swinging bat, I paused to gather my balance.

"Don't stop," Bo said. "They're close behind us."

Yes, my dog talks. He can speak out loud, but mostly his voice reverberates inside my head. We've become so connected that we can communicate and share thoughts without much conscious effort.

"I can see light ahead," he said. "Keep moving. I only need a little more space."

The trees were so close together that we had to dodge and weave through the stunted spruce and pine constantly. Dead branches blocked our path at every height, smacking into my body and various places and causing pain across my chest and thighs reminiscent of high school dodgeball. I managed to keep an arm raised to protect my face, and I wasn't sure if it was blood or sweat running down my forearm.

Every time a branch lashed across my cheek, it left fire behind, and every root underfoot threatened to pitch me forward into the muck. My breath came in ragged bursts, fogging in the cooling air. The forest swallowed the last of the daylight, shadows stacking on shadows until it felt like we were running blind into a throat of black. Zero stars on Yelp, I do not recommend.

Overhead, the canopy was so thick that there was no chance of sunlight reaching the forest floor. The lack of undergrowth made it easier than going through heavy brush, as long as we successfully avoided the murky pools of stagnant water that never seemed to dry up. A screech erupted behind us, and my chest froze up like I'd just inhaled a popsicle sideways. Which, by the way, is not how you're supposed to eat a popsicle.

I heard the terrifying, primal scream with my ears but felt it with my entire physical being. I spun so fast my goggles nearly launched into orbit. Because nothing says "you're about to die" like freezer-burn lungs and mystery banshees in the woods. My knees buckled, and every extremity in my body began to tingle as if no blood was flowing through my limbs.

I felt as though the very sound was attacking my heart, and it took all my willpower to keep moving. Most of the sounds become muffled in this dark, damp forest. This particular stentorian noise overcame the natural deadening of sound and felt as if it struck directly at the center of my soul. I'm sure Bo put in a little extra magical effort to help me overcome the effects of the creature's debilitating audio assault. A regular, non-magical person may have been frozen in their tracks, maybe even dropped dead from the power of the sonic attack.

It was more than fear; it was paralysis. The raw command of something old enough to know how to hunt men with sound alone. I staggered, clutching my chest, and Bo pressed his flank against me, his presence a lifeline. Sparks of his ancient power crackled against my mind, steadying me enough to push forward again. My legs felt like wet sandbags, but I forced them to move.

Reaching the edge of the stunted spruce-fir forest, we burst into a small clearing of exposed flat bedrock where there was no soil for anything to grow. The area wasn't more than a hundred feet across in a rough circle, but that was more than enough room for our needs. Bo turned back to face the tree line, exploding into his dragon form, crouched low in a battle stance. Smoke drifted upwards from his flaring nostrils. Bo was ready to defend us against whatever followed us out of the Katahdin woods as we waited on the exposed rocky surface.

Bo roared in his booming, gravelly voice, "Looks like it's dragon-o'clock!"

Despite the seriousness of the moment and imminent danger, I stifled a laugh.

"What did you just say?"

"I'm working on a catchphrase."

The sudden openness was dizzying after the claustrophobic trees, moonlight pouring down like silver floodwater across the rock. My lungs dragged in the fresher air greedily, but my relief vanished at the sound of the forest splintering just beyond the tree line. I could almost feel the weight of the creatures pressing against the border of the clearing, waiting for the chance to lunge.

We waited, my breathing hard and my heart pounding in my chest. Bo, my massive ancient dragon, waited to do battle. His scales shimmered in the moonlight, multiple shades of red reflecting the light of the nearly full moon. Many legendary and mythical creatures exist in the Maine woods, but only one dragon exists. Terra Draconis, the Earth dragon.

"If they come any closer, I will blast them into cinders," Bo assured me, smoke rising from his flaring nostrils.

Trees creaked, and limbs shattered and fell as the three beings chasing us for the last twenty minutes emerged from the edge of the woods. They stopped without stepping into the clearing. Three massively tall humanoid creatures stood silently. They looked like part of the forest, their bodies covered with leaves and twigs. The detritus of the forest floor camouflaged them almost completely until they stepped into the light. At a glance, I would have thought they were a tree. After that chase through the dense tree cover, I knew better.

They loomed, shoulders hunched, eyes like pits that reflected nothing. Their silence was worse than the chase. Their restraint meant thought, intelligence, and hunger were being held on a leash until they chose to break it.

These were Kiwakwa, according to Penobscot Indian legend, Maine's version of Bigfoot, but even more frightening. Enormous and shaped like a man, the Kiwakwa are cannibalistic. Legend says they have an unending appetite for human flesh and possess a heart made of ice. Their name means "walks about the woods," and that's precisely what they were doing until we stumbled into their territory.

Until recently, I didn't give legends like this a second thought. Stories are told around campfires to scare Boy Scouts on camping trips in Baxter State Park. Stories, that's all they were. Now I know differently. Now that my best bud is a dragon.

Bo's transformation into a dragon is an awe-inspiring moment, both terrifying and majestic at the same time. It's a moment when the illusion vanishes and the ancient power is revealed, hidden beneath his squat, drooling disguise.

Terra Draconis.

When Bo speaks in his true form, his voice booms like thunder across canyon walls. Darth Vader dragged through gravel and dipped in molasses.

In less hurried moments, the transformation is different. It begins as a slow ripple over his body like a breeze across a small pond, scales surfacing beneath fur, wings extending easily against his flanks. But in times of danger, it's a violent eruption of magical energy that no one who witnesses it ever forgets.

"Get on," Bo said to me in his deep and gravelly voice as he changed into Terra Draconis. "We should get back to the motel before dark."

A few seconds later, the clearing was a hundred feet below us, the wind whipping in my face and Bo's heartbeat pounding under me. I looked down as I pulled my goggles up onto my eyes and watched as the Kiwakwa slid back into the shadows of the forest that had always been theirs.

From above, the trees looked endless. All I could see was a quilt of black spruce and granite outcroppings stitched together by rivers of shadow. The Kiwakwa melted into it seamlessly, as if the land itself had made them. My heart still thumped in my ears, the echo of their screech lingering like ice in my veins. The night air bit cold against my cheeks, but it felt like freedom. For now, we'd escaped. For now, the hunt was over.

Only when the adrenaline stopped rattling my ribs did I notice him. Really notice him.

Bo's transformation isn't always explosive. In moments like this, when the fight is behind us, I can actually see the dragon hiding in plain sight. It starts with a low, guttural growl far too deep for a bulldog, a sound like the earth itself is clearing its throat. His jowls twitch, his skin rolls as if he's shaking off a swarm of invisible flies. Then his eyes ignite, brown turning molten gold, glowing like a forge.

The shift ripples outward: fur melting into hammered red scales, wings unfurling like sails. His stumpy bulldog tail lengthens and whips out behind him, spiked and serpentine with the weight of centuries. His face stretches, smoke curling from nostrils that weren't there seconds before. Drool and wrinkles vanish, replaced by a jaw lined with dagger teeth that could shred through steel.

What once looked like a dog becomes a creature out of storybooks and legends. Terra Draconis, the last of the Earth Dragons.

Still, I always see my same grumpy friend in those golden eyes. The same old Bo, who loves watching TV with me, and will absolutely steal my sandwich if I look away.

That's the trick. To the world, he's a myth. To me, he's just Bo.

CHAPTER TWO

IN THE BEGINNING

3 days ago. Saco, Maine

Red, John Patrick, and I are Protectors. We're part of an ancient order of wizards tasked with watching over a dragon's treasure and defending the world from any equally ancient dragon that could arrive to take the treasure back. Last summer, we failed. Jim died in the battle against Draco Marinus, and the empty chair in the corner still feels heavier than stone. I found myself glancing at the empty seat more than I cared to admit.

We were on the top floor of a converted old brick mill building overlooking the Saco River. The room has been a combination think tank and poker room for decades, as the three Protectors kept watch over the river below and the hidden treasure concealed nearby, sealed off in a cave.

The river roared faintly through the open window, moonlight silvering the ripples. Old rafters overhead creaked whenever the autumn wind picked up, and the walls smelled faintly of damp stone, pine smoke, and spilled beer. The poker table still bore faded rings from a hundred tankards, and a stack of mismatched playing cards sat abandoned at one corner, as if the Protectors had paused mid-hand a century ago and never bothered to pick it back up.

"Five disappearances now, and all during epic thunderstorms. It can't be a coincidence," Red mused as he paced back and forth across the wooden floor.

"Coincidences like that are as rare as hen's teeth!" John Patrick scoffed, his Scottish accent thick as damp peat. "Ye cannae tell me it's not the Thunderbirds behind this. It's them, sure as sunrise."

He slapped a meaty palm on the table, making the old wood groan, then picked up a tankard that looked old enough to have crossed the ocean on the Mayflower.

Ale sloshed inside, the scent sharp and yeasty. John Patrick's knuckles were gnarled as roots, scarred from centuries of battles I could only imagine. Yet his eyes, blue as the Saco River in spring flood, still burned with the fire of a man who had faced gods and come out cursing.

I was a little bewildered, so I didn't wait to ask my first question.

"The only Thunderbirds I know are a car Ford used to make, so could someone please fill me in? Grandma drove a Thunderbird when I was a kid, but I don't think it killed anybody."

Bo perked up from where he was lying on the floor, "Like that Stephen King movie, that was a good one."

My dog watches a lot of TV. It's a bad habit, but since he lived as a dragon for centuries before coming to me, I let him make his own choices. Bo spends most of his time disguised as a dog. That makes it a lot easier to get him into my apartment, anyway.

He scratched lazily at his ear now, pretending indifference, but I knew better. When the word "Thunderbird" was spoken aloud, his ears twitched, and a faint golden shimmer passed through his eyes. Dragons didn't like talking about other elemental beings, especially ones with wings.

Red turned from the window and walked over to the heavy wooden table where John Patrick was sitting. Sliding out a chair, he sat wearily. The last few days since the dragon battle and Jim's death had taken a toll on him. They are both over six hundred years old, don't look a day over eighty, and are as fit and healthy as most fifty-year-olds.

"Storytime, then," Red said as he propped his elbows onto the table and laced his fingers together.

"Maine's Wabanaki tribes have legends about the Thunderbirds. According to those legends, they are massive, supernatural birds that live on Mount Katahdin and control thunder, lightning, and storms. They punish anyone who does something to throw off the balance of nature. The Thunderbirds are the guardians of the sacred land around the mountain."

As Red spoke, his voice dropped lower, like the telling of the tale carried weight older than his years. The candlelight flickered against his lined face, deepening the shadows beneath his eyes. I noticed how his hand tightened unconsciously around the edge of the table. Protector or not, even Red held respect for these legends.

I did a little recap out loud, "Five missing hikers. None of them connected to each other, and they all disappeared at different times over the summer."

"But always during a wicked thunderstorm that came out of nowhere," John Patrick added.

The legends get a little more specific, and that's why we need to investigate," Red continued.

I pulled up a Penobscot legend on my phone: Pamola, the moose-headed, eagle-winged spirit who ruled storms on Katahdin. Guardian of the mountain. Revered, feared.

I let out a little laugh. "That's quite a description, sounds ugly."

"Ugly and dangerous, laddie. Verrrry dangerous," John Patrick muttered, rolling his r's like an engine refusing to start. "You'd be wise not to mock a beast like Pamola. He's nae just a moose with wings like the legend describes ... he's a guardian spirit, older than your tallest tales."

The room went still for a beat after his words. Outside, a gust of wind rattled the old shutters against the brick, and for a strange moment, it sounded like wings beating in the distance. I shivered despite the warmth of the hearth fire. Bo's eyes tracked the sound too, and that was what unsettled me most. When a dragon pays attention, you should too.

I thought about how fast my world had flipped in a few months. I used to be just a waiter pulling double shifts, with a weird knack for bending reality I didn't take seriously. Then the Protectors found me, and so did Bo. Turns out, my "knack" was wizardry, and my drooling bulldog was actually an ancient dragon. Now I wasn't just Wilder Blackwood, part-time server. I was Wilder Blackwood, Protector. And apparently, the guy who had to face sky-spirits and winged moose gods.

Bo stood up, stretched, and said, "Let's go."

"Go?"

"The mountain. How far?"

Checking the maps app on my phone, I saw it wasn't as far as I had previously thought.

"The closest town to Mount Katahdin is Millinocket. That's 215 miles from here. It will take three and a half hours to drive, and we aren't climbing a mountain in the dark to look for a mythical flying moose man," I said.

Red looked at me, "Be careful how you use the word mythical, Wilder. Remember, a few months ago, you would have said the same thing about a dragon."

"Legendary, then," I replied, reconsidering my language as I looked over at my little French Bulldog. "I'll go with that."

By now, Bo was walking in a circle around the table. He gets antsy sometimes, like a dog with ADHD. I know how he feels.

"I can fly faster than you drive."

John Patrick started laughing, his hearty voice filling the room.

"Out-thunk by a wee doggie!" John Patrick roared, slapping his thigh. "Och, we should let the mutt do all the plannin' from now on!"

Out-thunk by a wee doggie who is the only living dragon on Earth. Terra Draconis, disguised as a dog, has eight hundred years of accumulated knowledge. I don't feel bad about that at all.

"I appreciate that thought," Bo communicated only to me. We have a special mental link as dragon and rider, and it has come in very useful in recent times.

"Morning seems like a better plan," I said. "We'll get some rest and fly up there first thing. Bo and I will check out the area and come back to tell you all about it. Then, we can figure out our next step. Sound good?"

"Aye, laddie. Be careful, "John Patrick said as he stood up. "Be on alert for surprises."

The way he said it sent a shiver down my spine. A man who had lived through centuries of storms didn't throw warnings away lightly.

We all said our goodnights and went our separate ways. Back at the apartment, I began searching the internet for stories of

Thunderbird legends from indigenous Maine tribes and any additional information I could find about the missing hikers.

The glow of the screen lit my small living room, casting Bo's shadow against the wall in the shape of something far larger than a dog. His snores rattled softly, but every once in a while, his tail flicked as if he were dreaming of wings.

Ten minutes later, I was floored by the newspaper article I read:

THE MAINE LEDGER: Another Hiker Vanishes Near Katahdin — Rangers Baffled, Locals Whisper "The Storm Took Him"

Date: September 10th

Byline: Janine Watkins, Staff Writer

BAXTER STATE PARK, Maine — Search crews have suspended the search for 27-year-old Mark Dunwell of New Haven, Connecticut, who vanished last week while hiking solo along an unmarked ridgeline northeast of the Klondike.

Rangers reported sudden weather activity, including a thunderstorm that formed in under five minutes, forcing teams to retreat from the search area on three separate occasions. Nobody has been recovered. Searchers found Dunwell's backpack upright, dry, and zipped, with food untouched. His boots sat neatly side by side outside his tent.

"We're used to unpredictable weather," said veteran ranger Jack Shire, "but this wasn't natural. This was … targeted."

The Dunwell case marks the fifth disappearance in the Katahdin region since Memorial Day, all under similar conditions: sudden storms, missing persons, and no signs of struggle. Each incident occurred near or within the Klondike basin, an area considered sacred in Wabanaki tradition.

Penobscot elder Miriam Tomah, 84, offers a different explanation:

"The mountain protects itself. There's something older than any of us up there. Not evil—just watching. We called it The Wing That Brings Thunder. You climb too high with the wrong heart, and it carries you away."

Park authorities continue to warn hikers to stay on designated trails and avoid backcountry travel during unstable weather. No foul play is suspected.

Yet among the locals, another name is spoken in hushed tones:

"Thunderbird."

The words blurred in my vision as I reread them. An upright backpack. Boots neatly side by side. That wasn't how people vanished in panic. That was ritual. That was a warning. Bo snorted in his sleep, and I knew, even before he stirred awake, that the Thunderbird legend wasn't a story anymore. It was an address, and we'd just been invited.

CHAPTER THREE

A DOG DOING DOG STUFF

The area we flew in to is remote, possibly one of the most remote areas in the Northeast. The Klondike is a section of Baxter State Park that covers thousands of acres, with no roads or cell service. There's no calling for help for anyone lost or injured here unless they are one of the few who carry a satellite phone.

Flying over the Klondike is like looking down on another century. Vast carpets of spruce and fir roll out in endless green swells, broken only by silver veins of streams and black pockets of bog. From above, I could see where moose trails carved faint tracks through the thickets, paths so narrow they would vanish instantly to anyone on foot. It was beautiful, but it was the kind of beauty that reminded you how small and temporary you are. If you go down there, you disappear. The woods swallow you whole.

This vast backcountry is challenging to access and even more difficult to navigate. The thick undergrowth and wet ground make for a sloggy trek. Most hikers avoid this part of the park in favor of trendier hikes and climbs, such as Knife's Edge, one of the most unique views in America. Knife's Edge is a narrow, jagged ridge between Mount Katahdin and Pamola Peak, just over a mile long. Some have described it as walking a tightrope in the sky since the trail becomes as narrow as two feet with 2000-foot drop-offs on either side. It is breathtaking and terrifying at the same time. That geographical area was our original destination until we got sidetracked.

I'd looked at plenty of videos of Knife's Edge online before, but they don't do it justice. From the air, it looked less like a trail and more like the spine of some titanic sleeping dragon, its jagged plates rising against the clouds. One misstep there, and you wouldn't even have time to scream before the world claimed you. My stomach tightened just thinking about it.

The sky was clear as we flew over Baxter State Park, twenty miles from the closest town. Early fall in Maine can be a busy time for hikers and leaf-peepers in the park. There are 30 peaks within the 330-square-mile park, and right now, I'm concerned about every hiker and camper out there. This terrain is a bit too difficult for the two other Protectors to manage, so Bo and I are alone on this scouting trip. When we return to Saco tonight, I'll fill in Red and John Patrick on our findings.

The thought weighed on me. Alone. Yes, I had Bo, and he was basically a flying tank and wisecracking sidekick rolled into one, but I still felt the hole where Jim used to be. When you go from four Protectors down to three, the math gets a lot scarier.

We left early this morning and flew directly here. It's 120 miles as the crow flies or as the dragon flies, so that took us a little over two hours to travel. Bo could have flown faster, but there was no need to rush. I wore my long coat to stay warm since the morning autumn air was a bit crisp. A mid-morning second breakfast seemed like a great idea when we landed in Millinocket, so Bo transformed into a little brown French Bulldog, and we stopped at a diner I had read about on Yelp.

"Behave when we're in here, "I begged Bo. "Don't make people stare at me."

"I'm just a dog doing dog stuff," he replied. I could feel the mischievousness in his thoughts.

"Are you planning to pee on something or beg other customers for snacks?"

"I just want some breakfast. You don't need to worry about me making a mess on purpose."

That "on purpose" was doing a lot of heavy lifting, and we both knew it. The last time I trusted him in a restaurant, the chef nearly had a meltdown over a mysteriously missing roast chicken that had been cooling on the counter.

We grabbed the nearest Please Seat Yourself table and sat down. The waitress brought coffee within seconds and dropped off a menu.

"I'll be back in a sec to see what you and the furry one want, hon."

Bo was quick to mentally flash an image to me: donuts, pancakes, sausages, and a pile of scrambled eggs.

"Let's keep it simple, please," I offered to him. "You can't eat like you're at home."

He snuffed at me, a bit of smoke puffing out of his nostrils.

"Fine. Just three donuts. You get gassy."

I ordered the same and got a refill of my coffee.

The reviews about the donuts were completely accurate. It was also fascinating to read all the signatures on the ceiling of the Appalachian Trail from the thru-hikers who had signed their way to fame upon completing the long hike. Mount Katahdin is the northern terminus of the AT, so it's definitely something worth boasting about.

I craned my neck to read some of the scrawls. There were names from every corner of the country, doodles of boots, mountains, even one crude dragon that made me glance at Bo suspiciously. He only winked. It was strange to think that, for most of these hikers, the summit of Katahdin was the end of a journey. For me, it was looking more and more like the beginning of one.

I got a few sideways stares from judgy customers when Bo-cephus sat across from me at the table and ate a few donuts. It certainly wasn't normal dog behavior, but I didn't care what they thought. I finished my coffee, and Bo took a long drink of water from the collapsible bowl I had carried in my coat pocket. We then walked to the motel down the street, where I had booked a reservation online. I wanted to know exactly where it was in case we got back in town late that night.

"Did you find the section of Expedia that specializes in mo-tels that haven't been updated since Carter was President?" Bo jokes as we approached.

The Pamola Peak Inn was exactly what we paid for: a queen bed, a small bathroom, a desk, and a window overlooking the parking lot and mountain view beyond. I could cross the entire room of faded leaf-pattern carpet in four long steps, so it felt a little cramped. We had no intention of doing anything except sleeping there before we left for home in the morning, so the low-cost and pet-friendly room was perfect.

The walls smelled faintly of bleach and mothballs, the TV was one of those ancient box sets that hummed louder than it played, and the comforter was patterned with leaves that looked like they'd been designed in the 1970s. Still, after a morning of flying, I wasn't picky. Bo leapt straight onto the bed like he owned the place, circling three times before col-lapsing in a heap of snoring fur.

Naptime didn't last long. Avoiding observation and secu-rity cameras, we walked to the side of the building before Bo turned into the mighty dragon form that would take us to Knife's Edge for a look around the peaks. In seconds, the little French Bulldog underwent a massive transformation. I felt the power shifting through the air as Bo's red scales caught every available ray of sun and reflected them, giving him a red shimmer and glow that created a halo effect around him. My skin was buzzing with his energy. It was like downing six cups of coffee all at once.

"Sssssmokin'!" he hissed as he shook his head and neck.

"A Jim Carrey movie, really?"

The world's last dragon, and he quotes VHS tapes from before I was born.

Standing before me was Terra Draconis, fierce and majestic, ancient and powerful. Dragon magic keeps him concealed, so there is no danger of being seen. A dragon can only be seen if they want to be, except to any being with magical ability.

Even knowing that, my pulse hammered as his wings unfurled. A dragon in a motel parking lot felt like juggling dynamite in a fireworks factory. One nosy hiker with a GoPro and my entire life would become a YouTube conspiracy special. But Bo only grinned, smoke puffing from his nostrils like a man enjoying a cigar.

"Relax," he said in my head. "Humans see what they want to see." I hoped he was right.

Tucked in next to the Pamola Peak Inn, Bo crouched down, legs tensed and ready for the leap that would take us into the air. His wings extended, reaching wide across the well-manicured lawn. With one mighty leap, we were in the air, and with a few pumps of his mighty wings, we were quickly over the buildings and treetops, headed towards the mountain peak. Later, the maintenance man may wonder how those trash cans blew across the parking lot. Thankfully, they didn't hit any cars as they tumbled in the wind produced by Bo's wings. That's the thing about dragons: you can't see them, but the effects of their presence are undeniable.

The ground dropped away in a blur of rooftops and asphalt, and then only the forest stretched beneath us. All I could see was an ocean of trees rippling in the wind. The air stung cold against my cheeks, sharper the higher we climbed. I tucked closer to Bo's neck, the scales warm under my hands, thrumming faintly with power. From up here, Millinocket looked like a toy town on the edge of a great green sea, and Katahdin loomed ahead like the prow of a ship cutting through the sky. For a heartbeat, with the world spread beneath us, I forgot about missing hikers and thunderbirds and just let myself feel the freedom.

"The mountains whisper for me to come and I go."

John Muir

CHAPTER FOUR

THE SUMMIT

Flying on the back of a dragon is always exhilarating, no matter the time of year. Pressed back against the scaly ridge along Bo's spine as we climbed higher into the sky, I took a breath to appreciate the uniqueness of our relationship. Throughout unrecorded history, dragons and wizards have been adversaries. Dragons kill wizards, and wizards defeat dragons. Bo and I had a new and special symbiotic relationship. We can feel each other's feelings and hear each other's thoughts. We support and encourage each other wordlessly, and we are more powerful as a team than we ever could be individually. There has never been such a dragon and wizard relationship, and we both know how special it is.

The connection hummed between us, subtle as a heartbeat. I felt his calm when mine faltered, Bo's stubborn determination when my fear threatened to creep in. It was like riding not just on his back, but inside a shared spirit, a constant reminder that no matter how insane this mission became, I was never truly alone. The wind cut at my coat, cold and sharp, but under me was living fire, ancient and immovable.

Millinocket borders Baxter State Park and the North Maine Woods, three and a half million acres of forest land, most of it uninhabited and loosely connected by a series of logging roads and snowmobile trails. It's a moose-watcher delight, but we are searching for something far more extraordinary than the antlered behemoth that delights the fall leaf-peepers who come up here in busloads to see the colors of autumn.

From above, I spotted a pair of moose grazing near a pond, antlers wide as car doors. They looked up, ears twitching as if they sensed something vast passing overhead. Bo chuckled in my head, amused by how easily animals recognized him even through concealment. "They know better than most humans," he said. And he was right, nature always knows.

Leaving the motel behind us, we flew over the sites of former paper mill buildings, empty footprints of their former grandeur and productivity still visible on the ground from the air above. We soared high above the trees, northwest over Millinocket Lake toward Mount Katahdin. The sheer emptiness of the woodland below was astounding to me. I live in a small town, but this was true isolation. The North Maine Woods is one of the last significant wilderness areas in America. We rocketed over unspoiled forested areas of nature in its purest form.

I thought of Jim then, of how he would have marveled at this view. He'd been the one to tell me once that wilderness is not empty, it's full. Full of eyes, spirits, and memories that remember longer than people do. Looking down on the endless waves of pine and spruce, I felt that truth. It wasn't empty. It was waiting. Watching.

The colors of autumn were beginning to explode. Shades of red, yellow, and orange dotted the landscape below. Within a few weeks, this will be a kaleidoscope of colors and beauty, with not a single green spot visible except for the fir trees that rule parts of the landscape. Tourists pay beaucoup bucks to take bus rides through this area, but they still never get to venture this deep into the wilderness. Their expensive escapades are limited to the outskirts while never truly experiencing the depth of a true Maine autumn.

The air smelled different here. It was cleaner, sharper, and tinged with the faint sweetness of balsam fir. For a moment, I envied the leaf-peepers with their bus windows and cameras, safe and ignorant. They'd go home with stories of beauty, never knowing how close death might be perched above these cliffs.

The crisp fall air pinched against my cheeks, making me thankful for the goggles I wore. Thinking ahead, I had tucked a gaiter around my neck and pulled it up now as we flew to keep the chill off my face. My long wool coat kept me warm, but the sharp icicles of the wind hundreds of feet above the ground always find a way to squirm under my clothes to prick my skin.

We approached Knife's Edge Trail, over five thousand feet above sea level. The trail connects two mountain peaks and overlooks the Great Basin to the north. The Protectors thought this was the most likely place for the Thunderbirds to hide. The terrain isn't unlike the Swiss Alps. The vista is strewn with huge, barren rocky peaks of massive granite boulders, dotted with green spaces and low-lying lakes of icy water. The steep ascents and alpine-like tundra are similar to those found in mountainous areas in Europe, but without the presence of glaciers. Chimney Pond is a natural amphitheater encircled by dramatic high cliffs. Any of those steep and remote cliff areas could easily conceal hidden caves for a Thunderbird to roost. It would even be a natural area for a dragon to live, high above the world and far away from the annoyances and perils of civilization.

Bo's wings leveled us into a slow glide as we surveyed the ridgeline. I could feel his curiosity sharpen. Dragons respected high places, and I knew part of him longed to curl up in one of those caves, to pretend for a moment he was back in a world where his kind still ruled. The thought drifted across our link like smoke, tinged with sadness. I didn't comment, but I tucked it away. Even dragons dream of home.

The cloud cover came out of nowhere. What had been a clear blue fall sky turned into deep and dark bruises against a gray cloud cover, swirling in quickly and without warning. As the clouds increased, so did the thick mist in the air, almost a bank of fog half a mile above the ground. Visibility dropped to a few hundred feet in front of us.

"Bo, can you see any better with your dragon vision? You can usually cut through any fog and see better than I can."

"This is not natural. Fog does not do this. There is magic here. Blocks my vision."

"What are you saying?"

"Something is happening. To keep us away."

"From the mountain? But who ..."

His silence was more telling than words. I felt the low growl reverberate in his chest under my legs, an instinctive warning that even he didn't want to shape into language. Dragons rarely admitted fear. The fact that he wouldn't say it told me everything.

At that moment, the wind picked up to a gale force, throwing us unexpectedly to the side. Bo, buffeted by stronger winds than we had ever flown in, did his best to maintain altitude and flight control.

"Don't fall off," he warned. "Finding you would be hard."

That wasn't the kind of warning I wanted to hear. My hands tightened around the spikes on Bo's neck, knuckles whitening with the force of my grip.

The strong winds thwarted our approach to the mountain. Even a dragon can't fight a hurricane. With a massive crash, a bolt of lightning split the air to our right, and the rain began to pummel us. Bo veered left as quickly as he could, but we both felt the electricity in the air as it tickled my skin and caused my hair to stand on end.

"What the hell is happening? Are we under attack by something?" I asked as I dared to release my grip with one hand to swipe the rain off my goggles.

Bo's response was simple, "We are being kept away. From the mountain. Or by the mountain. Something felt us coming."

A fresh crack of thunder boomed so close it shook the marrow in my bones. I had the insane thought that the mountain itself had turned its face toward me. Katahdin wasn't just stone and earth. It was alive, and it wanted us gone.

Of course. There was no other reason for a cloudless fall afternoon to turn into a sudden thunderstorm with high winds.

We were both convinced we were dealing with a Thunderbird—maybe even the king daddy of Thunderbirds. Pamola Peak sits at the far end of the mile-long Knife's Edge trail, a razor-thin ridge connecting two summits more than five thousand feet above sea level.

The mountain takes its name from a genuine terror of Penobscot legend. Pamola, a nature deity, forbids humans from ascending Katahdin's peak. The summit is sacred, and intruders often meet with either danger or death. Pamola is the thunder god, the mountain's protector, and he wasn't just throwing a tantrum, he was trying to stop us from reaching our destination.

I'd mocked the description back in Saco: half-man, half-moose, half-eagle. Now, with the storm clawing at us, I wasn't laughing. I could feel the presence in every bolt, every shove of wind. This was personality, not chaos. Pamola wasn't legend. He was the landlord, and we were trespassers.

Bo twisted in the sky, wings thrashing against the blasts like a battleship plowing through a tropical storm. Lightning split and forked through the clouds all around us, and I realized too late that it wasn't random. These bolts had *intent*. They weren't just lighting up the sky. They were *aiming as* if Zeus himself was tossing a lightning bolt at us from Mount Olympus. Now I'm really mixing up my mythologies. Or realities.

Each flash came closer than the last. One exploded to our left, so close I saw the bones in my hands light up like an X-ray. The thunder hit a beat later, a gut-punch of sound that rattled my teeth and hollowed out my chest. I clung tighter to the spikes at the base of Bo's neck, every muscle in my body tensed like a bull rider intent on a prize-winning eight-second ride.

Bo let out a low, guttural roar. It wasn't the full-dragon war cry, but a warning, deep and old. I didn't know if it was meant for Pamola or just the sky itself, but the wind screamed back as if it had been offended. A powerful downdraft struck us hard, jerking Bo to one side. His massive wings lurched to correct, but the wind wasn't giving up. It twisted, pulled, shoved—like a dozen invisible fists trying to knock him out of the air from multiple directions at once.

We dropped a hundred feet in a blink.

The scream that tore from my throat was lost instantly in the storm. My stomach lurched into my throat, the world flipping sideways. For one terrible heartbeat, I thought I'd lose my grip entirely and vanish into the boiling clouds. Then Bo's claws flexed, his roar ripping the sky again, and the drop steadied into a glide. My whole body shook.

My stomach didn't get the memo. It stayed where we'd been, somewhere above the clouds, while the rest of me plummeted with Bo. Trees rushed up beneath us. At first a blur, then a threat, then *real*. Bo rolled at the last second, flattening his wings to cut the wind, and dove between two thunderheads like a fighter jet threading a canyon. I caught a glimpse of Mount Katahdin, impossibly distant now. A knife's edge, literally and figuratively, retreating into the storm.

We were being pushed north, away from the summit, away from our purpose.

Below, the landscape had changed. No more alpine ridges or rocky ledges, just endless green, dark and wet vistas broken by the occasional gleam of standing water. A spongy sprawl of mist and forest and bog stretched as far as I could see. This wasn't where we were supposed to land. This wasn't anywhere on our map, not even in the margins.

The Klondike. My gut twisted at the realization. Even saying the name out loud was enough to make old rangers shake their heads. The place was a maze of bogs and forest that chewed up compass needles and spit out bones. People didn't get found here. They just got remembered.

Bo banked again, grunting with effort, wings beating harder to keep us from crashing outright. The rain came at us sideways, cold and sharp as needles. I wiped water from my eyes with a half-frozen hand and tried to spot something—*anything*—familiar.

"This is bad," I muttered, though I doubt Bo needed the update.

No trails, no shelters, no sound footing. Just remote, unforgiving wilderness.

We were out of Pamola's reach... but we were also very, very alone.

Bo dropped lower, finally catching a break in the wind as we dropped below its influence, his wings stretched wide and steady now as we skimmed just above the treetops. Steam curled off his back where rain hit his scales, his body radiating heat like a living furnace. I could feel the tension in his muscles. He was tired and strained, but locked in. Focused. Determined.

He wasn't going to let us fall.

Not yet.

This was unquestionably not where we were supposed to be.

The storm still rumbled above us, Pamola's voice fading into the distance but not silence. It was a warning, a promise: we'd been spared, not dismissed. Whatever trial lay ahead in the Klondike, we were already inside his design. And I couldn't shake the feeling that the mountain was still watching.

Chapter Five

THERE'S NO PLACE LIKE HOME

After our Klondike adventure, if you can call it that, I needed a minute to think about what we had encountered. An ancient Wabanaki thunder god on the mountain, ice-hearted tree people who wanted to eat me, and amazing donuts. No joke, when we got back to the motel after the

Klondike freaks chased us through the woods, all Bo could think about was the next morning's breakfast.

"Diner and donuts?" Dragons don't scare easily.

"More donuts in the morning," I promised.

I was rattled. I wasn't about to admit that out loud but even sitting on the motel bed with the lumpy springs pressing into my back, I could still hear the echo of Pamola's storm in my bones. It wasn't just thunder, it was intention. Something about that realization wouldn't let me rest. Bo, of course, was stretched out and snoring like he'd just taken a stroll in the park. Ancient dragon, yes. Worrier? Not so much.

I was ready for a beer and some pizza, so I gave Bo a shake and asked the front desk clerk for directions. He sent us to a place down the street that was a little too lively for my tastes, but dogs were welcome. I don't know what it is about this town that readily accepts dogs sitting at the table with patrons, but I kind of like it. Maybe because they are so far away from anything else, they just don't give a crap.

"Order something spicy," he said into my head as we looked over the menu. "That Diavolo had chili flakes, pepperoncini, and spicy pepperoni."

For those keeping track, Bo likes pepperoni pizza. Most dogs probably don't, but the dragon taste buds take over, and he gets out of control.

"There isn't enough ventilation in the motel room if you have that for dinner. Plain pep is good enough."

"Life is too short to eat bland food."

"Says the dragon who has been alive for over eight hundred years. Settle down. We aren't on an episode of Diners, Drive-ins and Dives."

Frustration made the smoke curl from Bo's nostrils. He doesn't like it when he can't get what he wants. Dragons are used to being in control, after all.

The waitress gave us both a long look when the smoke drifted across the table. "Cold in here, huh?" she muttered, like her brain was trying to come up with any excuse besides the obvious. That's the thing about humans. They'll explain away anything that doesn't fit. A six-hundred-pound dragon could land in their driveway, and they'd blame the neighbor's lawn decorations. Bo smirked in my head, enjoying the joke I wasn't making.

The pizza was decent, the motel bed was lumpy, and the morning donuts were just as delicious as they had been the day before. My life is not routine. Proof enough is considering that after flying home on the back of a dragon, I was scheduled to pull a lunch shift at the restaurant back in Saco.

At home, Red's Riverside Tavern sits on top of a rocky ledge overlooking the Saco River, and my day job is working there as a waiter. The restaurant is located on the ground floor of an old brick mill building that has been converted into various businesses and offices. Also, there's a secret lair on the top tower floor where a trio of wizards keep watch over an ancient dragon treasure buried deep in a hidden cave on the island across the river. I know it sounds fanciful, but it's true. My ancient wizard friends, Red and John Patrick, have been here for a very long time. Their job as Protectors is to keep watch over the treasure and make sure no dragon can ever return to this world and regain possession. We averted a near-disaster last summer when the sea dragon, Draco Marinus, somehow crossed the barrier from the world he had been banished to and came searching for his treasure. Bo was able to defeat the other dragon and decided to stay here with me and the old dudes to essentially keep the world safe. That's the short version, anyway.

Sometimes when I walk into work, I wonder how Parker, my boss, would react if he knew his waiter's résumé included "dragon-slayer's apprentice." He probably wouldn't even flinch. He'd just ask me to run the fryer in addition to my tables. That's the kind of guy he is. Parker is unimpressed by danger and deeply impressed by punctuality. He's been through a lot in his life.

I donned my waiter apron and walked out onto the patio overlooking the river and saw my regular Saturday afternoon customers sitting at their tables, enjoying the September sunshine and talking excitedly to each other. They paused when I approached and greeted me with a smile.

"Hey, Wilder! Nice to see you again," blue-haired girl said from across the table.

The Maine Haunt Hunters were back for their weekly pancake breakfast. I still owe an apology to Parker, but it's one I can't explain. He bailed me out of a situation when I asked him to keep feeding endless pancakes to this motley crew a few weeks ago to buy me the time I needed to get ready to search for a mighty sea dragon. Now they keep coming back for the secret pancake menu item that doesn't exist.

Blue Hair Girl, Lanky Pancake Dude, and Chubby Tuxedo Boy are new regulars at Red's Riverside Tavern. Thanks to me, they come here before all their ghost-hunting adventures. Without them, I never would have found Draco Marinis, the sea dragon, a few weeks ago. They have no idea the absolute terror and destruction they inadvertently helped to avoid. I feel guilty that I don't know their real names, but it's easier to keep track this way. It's kind of like when the Starbucks barista gives a nickname on a coffee cup, but hopefully not in an insulting way.

"Hey, ghost gang!" I said as I smiled and brought their coffees. "Why don't ghosts dance at parties?"

Lanky Pancake Dude was the first to answer, sitting up straight in his seat like a proud second grader who knows the answer to the teacher's math question.

"Because they have NO BODY to dance with!" he said, as he laughed at his own joke.

"You got it! Sooner or later, I'll have a ghost joke you haven't heard before."

"Not likely," Blue Hair Girl said from behind her menu. "We've heard a lot."

"Pancakes all around again?"

"You know it!" Chubby Tuxedo Boy was lining up his fork and knife in front of him, and he tucked a paper napkin into the collar of his black and white tuxedo t-shirt. "I could eat stacks and stacks of these delicious little babies!"

He really leaned into that t-shirt tuxedo, too. Elbows squared on the table, napkin tucked just so, like he was about to dine at the Ritz instead of chowing down pancakes in a converted mill tavern. It made me grin. He treated every Saturday here like a holiday.

To be honest, they don't really eat that many pancakes. Occasionally, they'll order a second serving, but they'll all take one or two off the stack. Parker doesn't care, and he never asked me a reason why I needed them to stay at the restaurant longer. I'm fortunate to have his respect and trust. As a Gulf War veteran, he knows the value of those two intangibles.

"How did your YouTube episode down under the mill buildings turn out?" I was with them when they conducted their investigation, so I was curious to see if their equipment picked up anything at all. I'll admit to watching a lot of ghost-hunting TV shows sitting in my apartment at night. I was also curious if their EMF meters and spirit boxes accidentally picked up any evidence of a dragon in their midst while we were together, since Bo was also with us. Dragons put off a particular energy, but their magic usually makes them undetectable to any non-magic types.

"Our most popular episode ever," Blue Haired Girl said as she put her fork down. "We got a lot of DM's asking who our new member is."

"New member? Wait ... ME?"

They all laughed at the same time. Lanky Pancake Dude stabbed another flapjack off the stack in the middle of the table and dropped it on his plate.

"Not you, the dog! We made sure you were never on camera. Bo is now quite the internet star. The hashtag BocephusThe-Dog is even trending."

This is not good news. I don't want a bunch of internet trolls watching videos of my dog, in case they can catch anything "special" about him on video, and I have no idea what the video looks like. Magic can have a strange effect on electronics sometimes. For all I know, Bo could only appear as a flickering image, or even appear completely different on camera

I gently entered into the question phase of this conversation with a forced laugh.

"Haha, my dog is an internet influencer! What are people saying about him?

Not that he's secretly a dragon in disguise or randomly disappears on screen or has smoke curling from his nostrils for no apparent reason, please.

"It's mostly our female viewers," Blue Hair smiled. "They think he's cute and want to see more episodes with Bo in them."

Knowing how much Bo likes to watch TV when I'm not at home, I am one hundred percent certain he would absolutely love that idea.

"No way that can happen," I started to make excuses. "I'm sure he'll sniff, scratch, lick, or pee on something that you don't want on camera!"

Everyone laughed, and I hoped that was the end of that idea. I don't need a high-profile pet that isn't really a dog. The possibility of discovery increases greatly. We don't need a bunch of government secret-agent types poking around. We've managed to keep a low profile and only transform in areas without witnesses or security cameras. Any video would just show a little brown French Bulldog walking down the sidewalk and suddenly vanishing. We don't need any questions or internet conspiracy theories.

The images popped into my head anyway, tabloids with grainy photos of "Maine's Vanishing Dog." Headlines screaming about portals or cryptids. Bo would love the fame. I'd have to start changing apartments every two weeks, and I like where we live. It's convenient.

"Sad about that big brick smokestack," I redirected, looking across the river at the old factory smokestack that had been destroyed two months ago in a massive dragon battle that nobody remembers witnessing. Thank you, Protector magic.

"My grandparents both worked in that textile factory back in the day," Tuxedo Boy said as he shoved another syrup-dripping forkful into his mouth. "Grampa told me he climbed almost all the way to the top of that smokestack on the inside using some kind of access ladder built into it. He was going to put an American flag at the top when World War 1 ended, but the cops stopped him."

"Cool story, bro," Lanky Pancake Dude jabbed.

"It's true! He has just come back from France and served in the 26th Yankee Division. I remember because my dad still has a discharge certificate framed on the wall. Don't be a jerk, you know I love my family history."

"Almost as much as you love pancakes."

"Speak for yourself, you've eaten more than me!"

This was the typical banter I heard as this group sat around the picnic table out here on the deck overlooking the river. They were friends since elementary school, and nothing could ever come between them.

"I have more tables that need attention. Holler when you want the tab or more pancakes." It would be the latter, not the former.

I couldn't wait for this shift to be over so I could sleep in my own bed. Between the long flights back and forth to Millinocket and the turbulent flight around Mount Katahdin, then the run through the forest, I needed some better rest than the motel bed could provide.

Then my phone dinged and I read the text.

"Wilder, my sweet, weird waiter. I haven't seen you for three days."

Valerie. I texted her last night, but she didn't know about our trip up north. That's a little hard to explain, anyway.

"Hi, sandwich babe. Sorry, I've been a little busy almost getting killed by tree-creatures in the North Maine Woods, and saw my life flash before my eyes while flying in Baxter State Park." I thought it, but didn't type it.

Instead, I replied, "I miss you, too ...I have the day off to-morrow, how about lunch?

I stared at the screen a second longer than necessary, waiting for the three little dots of her reply. Nothing came yet. My stomach did that ridiculous teenage flip-flop it always did with her. I'd faced down sea dragons and storm gods, but somehow a single text from Valerie made me more nervous than any of it. Maybe because donuts and thunderbirds were temporary.

Valerie ... Valerie could be permanent. And that was scarier than any storm.

Chapter Six

PICNICS AND PUZZLES

September weather in Maine is as unpredictable as that of any other month. We may have four sunny seventy-degree days in a row, but the next day could be forty-five and rainy. When I knocked on Valerie's door the next afternoon to pick her up for our date, I was thankful it was a warm afternoon. Valerie decided we needed to have a picnic by the ocean.

"I'll go into the store and make them myself," she texted that morning. "Two Italian sandwiches with salt, pepper, and oil. Extra black olives on mine."

Of course, Bo came with us. He and I are practically inseparable except when I'm at work, but Valerie loves him, too. He clearly loves the attention he gets from her. The dragon and I have a bond that transcends the mental connection; it's also emotional. I can feel how much he loves it when she pets him on the head and strokes his ears. If only she knew she was petting an ancient not-quite-mythical dragon.

Bo and I walked the few blocks to Valerie's apartment, since I still don't own a car and she does. I think with my new sideline, I'm going to have to get something sooner or later. I can't always rely on flying on the back of my dragon to get somewhere. It's just not always convenient.

Valerie opened the door before I could knock again, keys in one hand, sandwiches in a brown paper bag in the other. She wore a soft gray University of Maine hoodie, jean shorts, and hiking boots. Casual and gorgeous. She smiled when she saw me, then knelt to greet Bo.

"Hey, handsome," she said, scratching his head. He closed his eyes in bliss.

"Told you he's in love," I said.

"With me or the sandwiches?" she smirked.

"Both, I think."

"I made an extra for him so we don't have to share."

Bo barked and wagged his stumpy tail like a normal dog might have.

"I think he understood me," Valerie laughed in her crazy, beautiful, quirky way. She tipped he head back slightly and flipped her hair over her shoulder.

If she only knew how well he understood her. That is one dog that will never have access to the bedroom when Valerie spends the night.

Watching her with Bo constantly stirred something strange in me. Comfort mixed with dread. I wanted to tell her everything, to peel back the curtain and let her see the truth about the dragon she was petting, the magic that curled around our lives like smoke. But the thought of her running, or worse, looking at me like I was a stranger, froze my tongue every time. For now, she gets to live in the safe version of my world. A picnic, a dog, a boyfriend. Normal.

A few minutes later, we were driving the fifteen minutes up the turnpike toward Portland. When we turned off the highway and crossed down to Commercial Street on the city's working waterfront, the sun was hanging low and softening to golden hour in the western sky on the city side. Valerie had planned it perfectly: a late afternoon ride on one of the Casco

Bay ferries, then a picnic on Peaks Island while we catch the sunset.

Portland bustled as always. There were fishermen hosing down decks slick with scales, tourists lined up for lobster rolls along Commercial Street, the smell of fried clams and diesel mixing in the salt air. Ferries rumbled like patient giants against their moorings. Valerie leaned forward as she drove, her eyes bright, pointing out little shops and murals like she was rediscovering her own city. I realized, not for the first time, how much she loved this place. She loved its grit, its stubbornness, and its heart. Maybe that was part of why I loved her.

By the time we laid our blanket on a stretch of grass near the rocky shore on the island three miles into the harbor, the view was like a painting. Fishing boats bobbed nearby, the scent of salt in the air, and the faint clang of a distant buoy bell echoed across the water. We had a million-dollar view of the city skyline set against a perfect Maine sunset. Fort Gorges sat halfway between the island and the city, in the middle of the harbor. It's an old Civil War-era fort, even though it never saw combat. The two-story granite fort is only accessible by boat, occupying the entire small island on which it sits. A short distance from Portland's waterfront, it's a popular destination for kayakers and explorers, since the island is also a city park.

The granite bulk of the fort seemed both stubborn and lonely, crouched on its little island with gulls wheeling above it. I'd been out there once as a kid. The place is rife with graffiti, weeds, the smell of brine in the empty casemates. My grandmother said the place was haunted by soldiers who never saw battle but carried the weight of waiting. Looking at it now in the amber light, I believed it.

We ate. We talked. We definitely laughed more than we should have. The bottle of wine we shared probably played a part in that.

Valerie told me stories from her childhood. She talked about summer swims at Crescent Beach, sneaking into drive-ins with her cousins, the time she broke her wrist falling off a rope swing and lied to her mom about it for three weeks. I countered with restaurant horror stories. Tales of customers who sent back perfectly good chowder, a guy who tried to pay me in arcade prize tickets from Old Orchard Beach, Parker's unshakable poker face when the fryer caught fire. Bo snored theatrically between us, like he couldn't believe he was missing out on the conversation. For an hour, maybe more, the world felt almost ... ordinary.

Without warning, something remarkable happened.

The color of the sky, once glowing with the bright hues of the sunset, darkened.

The wind changed direction with an audible *snap*, almost like a door slamming somewhere out in the harbor. Flags flipped direction, and boats in the harbor spun around and stretched their tethers in the opposite direction.

Bo sat up straight, ears perked. His head quickly turned toward the open bay, eyes on Fort Gorges. He growled with a low, uncertain sound I hadn't heard since we were underground in the Indian Island cavern searching for the sea dragon's hiding place.

Valerie looked up from her sandwich. "What's wrong with him?"

Before I could answer, the water in the bay *flickered*. That's the only way I can describe it. Like a shimmering ripple of heat over a hot road or a sheer curtain shifting in the wind. Far offshore, something massive surfaced, if only for a second. Not a whale. Too slow for a boat. And we haven't had a submarine sighting since Germany tried to sneak in a U-Boat during WWII.

The air tasted metallic on my tongue, sharp and unnatural. I felt the hair on my arms lift, the way it does before lightning. Somewhere deep inside, the part of me that has grown too used to magic whispered: This isn't random. I pressed one hand against the blanket to steady myself, but the ground seemed to hum beneath me, as if the whole island was reacting.

Bo's growl deepened, and his eyes glowed faintly golden, the inner dragon rising to the surface.

"Did you see that?" I asked. As Bo simultaneously said the same words in my head.

Valerie raised her arm to shield her eyes from the sun. "Something out there? Was it a seal, maybe?"

Bo's voice filled my head: "It wasn't a harbor seal. Something ancient and dangerous stirred beneath the water."

I stood, scanning the bay, my heart pounding. The water had become still again, just the gentle waves that would normally flow through the harbor. Empty, except for the usual fishing and lobster boats making their way back to the pier, ready to call it a day.

"Probably just a seal or something," Valerie repeated, lying back on the blanket. "We're in Maine. The sea's full of surprises."

Yeah, I thought. *You have no idea.*

But Bo knew, and now I knew. Whatever we just witnessed, even for just that moment, was a sign of something magical and ancient at work. Something was out there, hiding in the deep. Portland Harbor is the second deepest port on the East Coast, so there are a lot of places to hide.

I forced myself to sit back down beside Valerie, trying not to spook her, but my mind was already racing. Another sea dragon? A Thunderbird drawn to the coast? Or something worse, older, lurking beneath Casco Bay? My sandwich suddenly tasted like ash. Bo's thoughts brushed against mine, steady but grim.

"This isn't over."

I nodded, but only to him. Valerie laughed at a gull stealing a crust of bread from another picnic, oblivious. For her sake, I smiled and poured us the last of the wine. But my eyes kept straying back to the bay, to that shimmer in the water that wasn't supposed to be there.

"People who deny the existence of dragons
are often eaten by them."

Ursula K. Le Guin

Chapter Seven

HIDDEN DANGER

Valerie and I watched as the sun slipped behind the clouds, flooding the horizon with golden light. The moment had passed, but the feeling of dread didn't. I squeezed her hand, and Valerie looked up at me and smiled. I smiled back, but the fear that built up in me behind that cheesy grin was powerful and protective. I knew in that moment that I had fallen in love with her, and I would do anything to shield her from danger.

Somewhere beneath the surface of Casco Bay, something was watching. Watching and waiting.

We didn't talk much on the way to the pier to catch the ferry back to the mainland. Bo trotted quietly at my side, his head on a swivel as he was unusually alert. His cranium twisted constantly, eyes scanning the docks, the gulls overhead, the shifting patterns of the water. I could feel his tension like static electricity in my chest.

Valerie, cheerful as ever, didn't notice.

"I can't believe I haven't done this ferry ride since college, when we used to come here to the bar for Reggae Sunday," she said as we boarded. "I forgot how pretty it is out here. We should get a tandem bike next time, there's a rental place over there," as she pointed to a bike shop at the top of the hill before the downward slope to the dock.

"A bit difficult with a bulldog, but maybe we can find a baby seat he'll fit in."

Valerie and I laughed, but Bo seemed annoyed. The image in my head of Bo buckled into a baby bike seat was hilarious.

I didn't say anything more, but the thought of Bo with a tiny helmet and little aviator goggles made me snort so loud that a tourist gave me a strange look. Bo's mental voice cut back, dry as dust: "I dare you to try."

Once on board, we climbed to the upper deck of the ferry, where the breeze was stronger and the view stretched all the way to the horizon, past Fort Gorges in one direction and Portland Head Light lighthouse in the other. Bo sat next to us, head stuck between the railings for an unobstructed view.

We passed Fort Gorges, its granite walls mossy and lichen-covered, a massive silent sentinel of years gone by. Valerie leaned against the rail, pointing.

"I've always wanted to explore that place," she said. "It's so... eerie and beautiful at the same time."

"I can't disagree with you, something is haunting about the emptiness of it."

And it truly was always empty. Built before the Civil War, Fort Gorges never saw a single battle. By the time it was finished, the cannons designed to defend the harbor were already outdated. No garrisons ever marched across its parade ground, no troops slept in its dark casemates. It just sat there. Stone stacked against the tide, obsolete before it even had a purpose. Now weeds crept through the cracks, gulls wheeled over mossy walls, and every tide slapped against its foundation like a clock ticking away time. It was a fort without history, and somehow that made it spookier. Like it was waiting for something that never came.

I could feel something. A pull. Not from the fort, but beyond it or maybe even ... under it.

A few seconds later, the fort vanished from view. It was only a few hundred feet away from the ferry, but it disappeared. A fog bank that rolled in from nowhere socked us in a wall of thick cotton that blocked our vision of anything more than a few yards away. Turning, I couldn't even see the other side of the ferry, just 20 feet across from us.

The fog was heavy and dense, with an odd glow. Fog isn't supposed to glow, and this wasn't light from the moon overhead shining through the suspended water particles.

A shiver crawled up my spine. Valerie gripped my hand tightly.

Bo's voice crept into my thoughts. "It's the same fog. From last summer."

I didn't need him to explain. I remembered it well.

Last summer, before we faced Draco Marinus, a similar fog bank had materialized from nowhere off the coast, although that time it wasn't glowing. Some kids had become lost on their little sailboat somewhere offshore of one of the hundreds of islands in Casco Bay. The Coast Guard couldn't get out in the thick fog, and it was up to yours truly and his magic dragon who isn't named Puff to find them. Mission accomplished, and nobody was any wiser about there being a massive freaking dragon flying overhead.

"Valerie," I said carefully, "do you see that fog?"

She turned, eyes narrowing. "Huh. That's weird. It was clear just a minute ago."

The ferry captain's voice crackled over the boat's PA system, "We'll be docking shortly, but due to the low visibility, we are slowing our speed. I'll be honest, folks. I've never seen fog like this in Portland Harbor."

Nor reassuring.

After a moment, he continued. "We're going to stop engines and wait here for a few minutes to see if this fog clears a little bit. I'd hate to run over another boat stuck in this mess."

The engines wound down into silence, and the chatter of passengers hushed with them. Water slapped hollowly against the hull. Even the gulls had gone quiet. It was like the whole harbor was holding its breath.

The fog kept moving, unnaturally fast considering there was no breeze to carry it along. It didn't roll in and out like usual coastal fog. It moved deliberately and slowly, like a predator stalking prey. Purposeful and planned. I could feel the malevolence it contained, and Bo echoed my thoughts.

"I don't like this," I said under my breath, hoping my imagination was getting the best of me.

Bo growled softly. "Testing the barrier."

"What barrier?" I asked him silently.

"The boundary between their world and ours. Something's trying to break through."

I looked back toward the fog. It was denser now, if that was even possible. Even the seagulls had gone silent. The distant foghorn from Two Lights State Park was silenced in the sound-dampening thickness.

The whole scene reminded me of a Stephen King story called The Fog, and that didn't end well.

Then I saw the shape.

For just a second, lost in the mist as thick as a cotton ball in an aspirin bottle. Were those ... wings? They didn't move. Whatever it was seemed to be here, but not here at the same time. I blinked, and it was gone.

Bo's head whipped toward me.

"Did you see it?"

I nodded once.

Valerie glanced back at us from her spot on the railing. "Hey, are you okay? You look like you just saw a ghost."

"I wonder," I said under my breath. "Hey, they started the engines again!"

Sure enough, the fog was thinning quickly, and visibility had increased to a hundred feet in only a few seconds.

We pulled into the dock ten minutes later, but everything had changed. The air was colder. Fingers of fog gripped around islands in the bay as it retreated. Even the other passengers seemed a little thrown off by the experience, probably because the strange twist in the weather had ruined all their selfies out on the water.

Bo stayed right next to me, eyes locked on the water beyond the ferry.

"Whatever is coming hasn't arrived yet," he said. "But it's close."

That's when I spotted the three familiar figures waiting on the dock with camera bags and tripods. The Haunt Hunters.

Blue Hair Girl perched on the pier railing, filming a TikTok intro. Lanky Pancake Dude was fiddling with a camera that kept shutting off. Tuxedo Boy struggled to carry a cooler in one hand and a Dunkin' box in the other.

"Fog like that?" Blue Hair announced to her phone. "That's gold. Fort Gorges at night is gonna look like *Silent Hill*."

"Only with worse snacks," Tuxedo Boy grumbled, wiping off the powdered sugar dusting his shirt.

"Ghosts love this stuff," Lanky Pancake Dude insisted. "Look, my EMF meter is already spiking." The device's low-level hum quickly ramped up to a high-pitched squeal, causing nearby tourists to plug their ears and give nasty looks toward the trio. The meter let out a long beep and died in his hand. "Aw, come on!"

"Classic," Blue Hair grinned. "The spirits always drain our gear."

I plastered on a smile as Valerie saw the kids. "Hey! It's those ghost-chasing kids again. Small world."

"Small haunted world," I muttered.

Bo's low growl vibrated through my chest. Not spirits. Not harmless. Not a joke.

The Haunt Hunters, blissfully unaware, were heading out into the dark on their own little adventure. Straight toward a danger even they couldn't imagine. Now that the fog had lifted, I had no reason to stop them.

CHAPTER EIGHT

BREAK ON THROUGH TO THE OTHER SIDE

"**B**o, we've never talked about how you got here," I said, looking across my apartment at the little brown French Bulldog that is secretly a massive red Earth Dragon.

"You don't remember? You set a bag down by the front door. I tried to steal your groceries."

"Not that. Of course, I remember that. It was the first time in my life that a dog spoke out loud to me. And stole my Twinkies. Definitely memorable. I mean ... how you got here from the other side. Beyond the veil, or whatever that is."

"Where the Protectors banished the remaining dragons six hundred years ago."

"Yes, are you still mad about that?"

"If I was, this city would be a toasty pile of rubble."

I looked at him in silence for a moment, until his laugh finally broke the mood. If you think a canyon-deep gravelly voice coming from a dog's mouth is odd, you should hear him laugh.

"Ha ha ha, don't worry. I like this place. Friends. My new role with your Protectors is better than fighting and killing for centuries. I wish we had started to work together sooner."

"I agree," I replied, grabbing another Coke from the fridge and making a note on a Post-it to buy more at the store.

"But world-domination and search for treasure made it impossible."

Again, just enough silence to make me turn my head and give him a stare before the laughing began. I could feel his emotions surrounding the banishment in his thoughts. The "other side" where the Protectors banished the few remaining dragons, is a desolate and depressing place, even for a dragon. Images flashed in my mind's eye, making it clear that there's nothing to do except fight for your life against the other creatures who live in that dimension.

"Eventually, all the dragons besides Draco Marinus and me killed each other. I had the land. She had the sea. Impasse."

"Wait ... she?"

"You can't tell what a girl looks like? You should date more. Good thing you have Valerie now." More laughter.

"Okay, okay. Very funny. But seriously, I didn't know that. Can we get back to you and your arrival, please?"

Bocephus trotted across the apartment and hopped up onto the couch. It was one of his favorite spots since it has a nice view of the street below. While I'm at work, you can usually look up into my third-story apartment window and see him watching the comings and goings below while leaving a drooly mess on the windowsill. It's a daily cleaning job for me.

He sat there now, chest rising and falling in slow rhythm, as though marshaling the right words. His eyes, those molten, golden dragon eyes hidden beneath a bulldog's droop, fixed on nothing as they became lost in memory. When he spoke, his voice was softer, more deliberate than usual.

"The other side, or other world, is eternally in twilight. Nothing of substance grows, only blackened stumps of trees on rocky outcroppings. Deep valleys crisscross the land, their depths best left unexplored. No water, apart from one small sea. Draco Marinus ruled there since the time we were the newcomers in that strange land. She was the largest and most powerful in the water. No other sea dragon from this earth existed in that land."

The picture sharpened in my mind, carried on our link. I felt the grit of ash on my tongue, smelled the metallic tang of a world where nothing lived. The sky was not black, but bruised: a permanent twilight where the sun never set yet never rose. Gray light seeped through the air as though filtered through smoke. Shadows didn't stretch, they just ... clung. Bo's memory pressed harder. There were ruined forests reduced to skeletal stumps, roots clawing at soil too thin to feed them. In the distance, valleys yawned wide, their bottoms invisible. The thought of falling into one of those voids made my stomach twist. Even Bo's dragon mind recoiled from the depths.

A clear image formed in my mind, Bo's memory of his time there. He flew above a rocky area, and massive outcroppings of black stone jutted above the thin soil. He flew further, massive red wings pumping hot air behind him, driving him further into a land no human could ever survive. The Earth Dragon glided over the beginnings of a fetid swamp, the air filled with the stench of death and rot. His nostrils flared as he inhaled and rejected the gas and fumes expelled by the swamp below, not knowing whether it was poisonous or not.

In the air ahead of him, Bo saw a bright blue clearing open up, almost as if a circular window was floating hundreds of feet above the swamp. It was dim at first. He pumped his wings harder, flying faster as curiosity won out over intellect. Eventually, as he drew closer and the portal expanded, it was at least a hundred feet wide. Hanging in the air above the quagmire below.

"I love danger. I flew into it."

He paused as if waiting for me to ask questions. I had none, so the story continued.

"After hundreds of years in a world of constant near-darkness, the light and color were impossible to resist. I passed through."

His words dripped into my mind like water after drought. I felt his awe. Sunlight blinding after centuries of gray. The roar of the wind was clean in his ears instead of the stench of rot filling his nostrils. For him, it was like a drowning man breaking the surface.

"Then I was here."

And though he said it with the bluntness of a soldier, beneath the gruff tone I felt something else. I felt the relief. Maybe even wonder. The brain movie continued. In a heartbeat, Bo went from flying over a world on the brink of life into one that was filled with it. He came through the portal over water into a clear blue summer sky.

"Near where we were today. On the boat."

"When we had the picnic with Valerie? Did anyone see you? I'm sure there would have been someone posting on social media if they saw a huge red dragon flying over Casco Bay!"

"I'm not dumb. Vanished a moment after I crossed over. It could be dangerous. Best to be unseen."

"And then?"

"I flew. Over land, to the south. I began to recognize ... oddities under me. The land was familiar. This world and the other side are the same. The same world. Two sides, same coin."

I slammed my Coke down on the coffee table, fizzing and splashing. Another mess for me to clean up later. "What do you mean?"

"The other side is a magical creation. A prison of sorts. A dark mirror version of this world. Where there is an ocean, I have seen a black and deadly swamp. Stretching on for a thousand miles. Where there are lush green forests and farmland here, there is only scorched earth and blackened stubs of trees."

Bocephus was using more words to communicate than I had ever heard before. His sentences are usually short and succinct.

"A shadow of this world," I said.

"That world is this world, created and held in place by ancient magic. Even older than the Protectors. Magic so ancient that the giants were walking this earth. When the old gods reigned supreme, they needed somewhere to send their enemies if they couldn't defeat them."

My chest tightened. The scale of it was crushing. The Protectors seemed ancient to me, but what Bo described stretched back before recorded history, even before the dawn of myth. Gods shaping entire dimensions not to destroy their foes, but to cage them. I tried to picture it. Spells not like mine, but titanic workings laid into the bones of the earth, a whole world folded against itself like a shadow. And inside it, dragons and who knows what else. Trapped. Waiting.

I sat silently for a few minutes, contemplating this massive thought.

"The energy this would require ..."

Bo chuffed. "The earth provides power. There is no short-age. The spell is unfathomable, not the source of power."

"Back to your ... how did you end up on my doorstep?"

"Instinct. I followed. It pulled me to you."

I understood. "You felt me, a wizard. There was a connec-tion, and you followed the thread."

"Thought about eating you. Good thing you had snacks. I was hungry."

I waited for another laugh at his latest joke, but one didn't come.

"Kidding," he woofed as he jumped off the couch. "Need to go out."

He padded to the door like any other dog, nails clicking on the wood. But I couldn't shake the echo of what he'd told me. Two worlds. Our everyday world and its shadow. A prison stretching back to the dawn of the gods. A dragon drawn through a strange portal by instinct, by fate, by me. And now he wanted to go outside for a walk, as if nothing had happened.

CHAPTER NINE

WHEN IN DOUBT, ASK AN OLD MAN

I texted Red to let him know Bo and I were headed for the park. Red and John Patrick often like to join us on our walks together. It's a good opportunity to talk about our group and make plans for the future. We've been a little off our game since the sea dragon in the old mill catacombs killed Jim. After so much time together, the shock to the surviving duo was a huge mental blow.

The Thesauri Custodes, or Protectors, are a trio again, thanks to my inclusion. No Thesauri Custodes have ever had a dragon on their team, so we are one of the most powerful wizard gangs on the planet. Truth be told, nobody knows where the other Protectors are, or even if any survive.

The park was one of those green spaces where times slowed down enough for you to enjoy the day without worrying about tomorrow. Massive oaks shaded benches carved out of local stone, the kind with bronze plaques bolted onto the back in memory of people whose names sounded like they belonged in Revolutionary War diaries. Children shrieked at the playground on the far side, the sounds carrying faintly over the burble of the Saco River. The smell of hot dogs from a nearby vendor cart mixed with the scent of damp leaves. Early September is the beginning of summer's end. I could already see the tips of some maples turning, tiny red warnings of the firestorm of color to come.

"Hey gang!" I shouted as we arrived at the park and approached the men on the granite bench. They hate it when I call them that.

"I hate it when you call us that," John Patrick replied in his thick Scottish brogue. "Ya need to stop doing that, laddie."

"Never," I laughed in a jab-your-buddy-with-an-elbow sort of way.

John Patrick couldn't take the ribbing. "We are not a GANG. We're wiz ..."

He stopped himself just before Red's hand slapped in front of John Patrick's mouth.

"I need to take a whiz," Bo barked. To anyone nearby, he only barked. The words were clear inside our heads. Dog comedy.

"Very funny, wee little doggie, very funny."

"Don't encourage him," I laughed as I sat down on the bench with them.

Red let out a hearty belly laugh, as big and bold as his six hundred years have earned.

"I don't think that one needs any encouragement at all, Wilder! He's a free spirit, and an old one at that. If you think we're old, remember he's been around a few centuries longer."

Bo walked past us and nonchalantly chided, "But I look better for my age."

We all got a good laugh out of that one, then settled back for a talk.

"Bocephus has a theory, and I want your thoughts, "I began. "After so many centuries banished to the other side, he believes he knows exactly where that is, and how it was created."

"Laddie, nobody knows that, because nobody has ever been there and back."

"I was there," Bo reminded as he sat on the grass in front of us, tongue lolling to one side. "Now I'm here."

Stunned silence.

"Och, that's true. If that's where you came from. Why haven't we talked about this before?"

I jumped in before Bo could make a smart-ass comment. "We've been a little busy fighting an ancient water dragon and saving the planet from destruction. And then we were in a period of mourning. Now we can talk about the facts facing us."

Red stood up and paced back and forth, something he almost always did during our chats. Red needs his feet to be moving for his wheels to get turning.

I watched him, hands clasped behind his back, boots grinding in the gravel path as he moved like an old general preparing a war council. His red beard, streaked white, caught the shifting light as a gust bent the treetops. John Patrick sat heavily, as though rooted, his expression skeptical but curious. Being the youngest, it always struck me how strange it was to be partnered with them: two men carrying the weight of centuries, and me, a guy who still forgets to buy groceries if I don't write them on a Post-it.

"So Terra Draconis started here on our Earth, in the times of our fore-fathers, when there were knights and dragons and damsels in distress. When the Protectors defeated most of the dragons, those that remained were magically banished to another dimension not far removed from our own. Similar, but not connected."

"That's what you've taught me," I interjected. "But I think Bo has figured out even more.

"That Shadow Earth isn't only reached by magic; it was created by magic. Magic older than recorded history."

I told Red and John Patrick about Bo's surprising short journey here. Up until this point, we were only focusing on the fact that Bocephus had appeared here and not worried about the means of his arrival. Nobody ever asked the questions, so Bo never provided the answers.

"A portal of some kind?" Red proffered.

"A magic doorway from that world to this one." John Patrick suggested.

"I think it might be connected to the return of the Thunderbirds. It's a wild theory, but maybe whatever opened the portals that let Bo and the sea dragon through is also affecting other magical beings that have been slumbering for a thousand years."

"That's a wee stretch of the imagination, dontcha think?"

"Not at all," I defended. "I think there's some odd, possibly even magical, activity happening somewhere in Casco Bay, and the side-effect is the awakening of long-dormant beings that gave up their place in this world long ago."

Both went quiet at that. The kind of silence that comes from men calculating possibilities, measuring a younger wizard's theory against centuries of lore. The only sound was the whisper of leaves turning over as the wind stiffened.

Red had stopped pacing now, arms crossed as he gazed at the darkening sky. The clouds had thickened, the light shifting from late-afternoon golden hour to the bruised purple of a storm's arrival. His silhouette against that backdrop made him appear older, almost as if he were carved out of stone. It hit me that six centuries of weight rested on those shoulders. Six hundred years of battles fought and won. And yet, somehow, he still had the strength to stand here and plot the next move.

John Patrick, on the other hand, leaned forward on his elbows, the granite bench groaning under his bulk. His thick fingers tapped against his knee as if impatient, like a blacksmith waiting for iron to heat. He was skeptical, sure, but I'd learned something important about John Patrick since I joined them: skepticism didn't mean dismissal. It meant he was considering every angle, waiting for the one chink in the armor that proved or disproved a theory.

"Tell me this, laddie," he said at last, his brogue rolling like distant thunder, "If the veil was created, as yer doggie here claims, then who in the nine hells had the power to make such a thing? Ye say 'older than recorded history.' That covers a fair bit of ground."

Bo's lip twitched, smoke curling faintly from his nostrils as if the thought itself irritated him. "Older than your kind," he replied flatly.

Red cut in, his tone measured. "You mean the old gods."

The words dropped heavy, like a stone tossed into deep water. I didn't even know which old gods he was referring to. Greek? Norse? Wabanaki spirits? Something earlier still? For a second, the world around us felt thinner, as if the mention of them tugged at the threads holding reality in place. The storm overhead cracked faintly, a rumble without lightning, as though the sky agreed with Red's conclusion. Or was it something more?

Bo didn't answer immediately. His eyes, dog eyes to anyone else, dragon eyes to me, shifted toward the clouds. "Not gods," he said slowly. "Forces. Names came later."

Red only nodded, stroking his beard. "And if those forces made the Other Side a prison, then the cracks we're seeing, the fog at the fort, the storms on the mountain, they aren't accidents. They're fractures. And something is straining against them."

The maple leaves around us rustled louder than before, silver bellies flashing like fish. A jogger passed on the path with earbuds in, oblivious to the way the sky darkened further. The normalcy of it struck me. Two octogenarians and a bulldog discussing cracks in the magical fabric of reality while life in Saco continues with picnics, strollers, and joggers. If only they knew.

Hearing my thoughts, Bo turned his head toward me. "It is always like this. Storms gather. The world walks blind."

"Cheerful," I muttered.

Red resumed pacing, boots crunching the gravel, voice picking up energy. "If this is true, if the barrier is fraying, then the Thunderbirds may not be choosing to return. They may have been forced. Spirits bound to a place, suddenly untethered."

John Patrick jabbed a finger in the air. "And if they're untethered, they'll lash out. Ye saw it yerself, Wilder. Pamola was flingin' storms at ye like rocks at a sinner. If they don't trust us, they'll see every soul on Katahdin as trespassers."

I swallowed. I'd seen what Pamola could do from the back of Bo's neck. Lightning aimed with precision, winds like invisible fists. The idea of those storms unleashed without control made my stomach knot. Hikers, campers, and whole towns on the fringes of the park were in danger. It wasn't just our fight anymore.

Bo stretched out on the grass, unimpressed by the storm above. "Pamola tests you. He has not chosen yet."

"Tests me?" I asked.

Bo's golden eyes glinted. "Protector. Dragon's rider. Lover of mortal girl. You walk too many paths. He waits to see if you can hold them."

That shut me up. Bo didn't usually get poetic, which meant when he did, he meant every word. The weight of it sat on my chest, heavier than the thunderclouds rolling in.

Red stopped pacing and turned to me. "Then we prepare. The veil may be cracking. The Thunderbirds may be restless. And if Pamola himself is watching you, Wilder..."

He paused, eyes narrowing. "Then you'd better be ready to prove yourself. Not just to him. To yourself."

The wind had shifted in the last few minutes, and it looked like clouds were rolling in from the west for a thunderstorm. The maple leaves flipped upside down on the branches, a sure sign that the wind had shifted direction and a storm was approaching. That's not magic, it's Boy Scouts. I learned a few things during my years as a scout, including that I was the best at starting a campfire. That part really was magic, though. I never told my parents that the award I won on that camping trip was due to anything other than my skill with a single match. The memory flooded back to me in an instant.

The boys in Troop 310 had been out on a week-long camping trip. We weren't far from town, but for some of the boys, it may as well have been on the moon. No cell phones allowed. After we set up our tents and prepared the camp, the Scoutmaster announced the fire-building contest. We split up into groups of three, and each group was instructed to gather our kindling and firewood. He set up a string attached to two sticks, with the string three feet above the center of where we needed to start our fire. The first group to start their fire and burn through the twine would be declared the Firestarters and take home the three little whittled trophies.

The Scoutmaster blew the whistle, signifying the beginning of the contest. The groups scattered, each running through the underbrush to gather the combustible materials needed to start a good blaze. It was me, Teddy, and David in one group. We had been friends since third grade and were also on the cross-country team together.

Arms loaded with kindling and larger dry wood to burn, we threw it all down next to the fire pit as we dropped to our knees, feverishly building the proper fire. A little pile of birch bark to light, kindling on top of that. The branches above grew progressively larger until there were a few as thick as our arms crisscrossed on top. That's the one-match challenge. Build it, light it, and hopefully coax it to burn with some extra oxygen as we gently blew into it, giving life to the flames.

None of that extra work was necessary, though. We quickly built the fire, and I flicked our single match off one of the rocks encircling the fire pit for safety. As I pressed the burning match into the center of the kindling, prepared to watch it light the birch bark, a small gust of wind blew through the site, extinguishing the match and ending our only chance at success.

In my mind's eye, I imagined the match still lit and igniting a huge flame instantly in our well-built stack of wood. In an instant, before Teddy and David even noticed the match had gone out, the bark exploded into flame, reaching a foot high in three seconds. The Scoutmaster, hearing the sudden whoosh of burning kindling, turned just in time to see the orange, red, and yellow flames lick the biggest wood on the top of the stack. Hot fingers of fire leapt upward toward the string, and in less than ten seconds, the contest was over.

"I've never seen a fire go up that fast," he said, blowing his whistle in three short bursts. "Game over!"

I could still remember Teddy's wide eyes, the disbelief on David's face. Nobody said anything in the moment, but I knew what I'd done ... or at least, what I'd caused. Magic had cheated for me, flaring at the edges of a boy's desperation. A spark not from a match, but from me. That fire burned in my memory as much as it burned the string.

When I finished telling it, Bo yawned exaggeratedly and rolled onto his side in the grass.

"Figures," he said into my head. "You've been cheating since you were twelve."

His tail thumped once, smug. Red chuckled. John Patrick only shook his head, muttering something in Gaelic I couldn't quite catch.

CHAPTER TEN

HIKING IS NOT FUN

We needed to go back. Back to Mount Katahdin. Back to searching and exploring the surrounding area. Our focus this time was Chimney Pond. I know there's something to find up there, something worth looking for. The high cliffs that tower over the pond in the basin make it a perfect aerie for the Thunderbirds. I have a sneaky feeling that the massive bowl formed by glaciers and encircled by those dramatic high cliffs is soon going to host a big show.

"We can't go in the same way we did before," I said to Bo. "We'll fly up to Millinocket and get a room at the motel again."

"And more donuts."

"Yes, of course. Always donuts. We're going to have to hike the rest of the way so we don't draw any unusual attention from whatever is up there protecting the mountain."

"Look at me. Stubby legs." Bocephus lifted each of his legs in turn, as if to display their limitations.

I rolled my eyes. His squat bulldog legs looked ridiculous as he raised them one at a time like a toddler showing off new shoes. His pouty face completed the performance. I'd seen knights in medieval murals look more dignified in battle than my dragon disguised as a loaf-shaped dog, whining about cardio.

"The hike isn't too bad. We'll borrow Red's truck for the drive up, and then it's only a few miles' drive from the motel to the trailhead. After that, we'll hike. I checked my hiking app, and it shows a distance of just over 3 miles. We can make it in less than two hours, even counting rest stops for your stubby legs."

"Bring snacks."

"I'll pack all the necessities, including snacks. We don't want to end up lost and needing a rescue."

"We can fly."

"Oh, right," I laughed. Occasionally my brain just won't acknowledge that little fact. Sometimes in my head, I'm just a waiter with a dog. Other times, I'm a wizard with a dragon for a best friend.

"Dogs aren't allowed on the trail, by the way. So be prepared to disappear if we run into anyone else. The app says it's a popular hiking spot."

Bo snorted, "Humans are dumb. Dogs are the best."

"Yeah, but you're not really a dog," I muttered under my breath.

"Blasphemy," he shot back in my head, then proceeded to lick his paw with exaggerated innocence.

I texted Valerie and told her that Bo and I were going hiking in Baxter State Park for a couple of days. She said she'd be working all week anyway, and to have a fun trip without her. She also said to stop by and she'd pack us some sandwiches for the hike, and I'm not going to pass up that offer.

"You boys stay out of trouble and be careful up there," she said when we arrived at the shop. The look of concern on her face was unmistakable. "There's been too many disappearances, and I don't want anything to happen to you."

"Don't worry about us," I reassured her. "Bo can have a fiery temper sometimes when he doesn't get what he wants. I feel safe with him by my side."

She laughed at the joke, even though it was the truth. Valerie leaned over the counter to kiss me before Bo and I headed out the door to Red's truck, which I had left parked out front on the curb in a 15 Minutes or Less spot.

The truck itself was an antique beast with faded red paint, a dented driver's-side door, and a dashboard that smelled permanently of pipe smoke and motor oil. Bo claimed the passenger seat instantly, circling twice before plopping down with a grunt that shook the springs. Every mile up I-95 north was a reminder of how long Maine really is. Towns grew fewer, gas stations farther apart. By the time we passed Medway, pine swallowed the horizon in every direction.

Bo's head was out the window half the time, lips and jowls flapping in the wind like a basset hound in a car commercial. Every so often, he'd shout into my head over the roar of the highway: "Moose!" "Donuts!" "That smells like bacon!" My response was usually, "That was a skunk, genius," or "We can't stop at every Dunkin." We made it in one piece, though my ears were ringing from his constant commentary.

Fast forward through hours of driving with an annoying dog shotgun rider, and another three hours of hiking with the same annoying companion, and we were standing at the precipice of 2000-foot granite cliffs looking down at Chimney Pond in the middle of the Allagash Wilderness. It had taken us an hour longer than we expected, but our view was astounding. Maine at its most raw and vulnerable. A postcard of this view could just as easily be labeled as the Swiss Alps, the Pyrenees mountains in France, or the Colorado Rockies. The sun was reaching mid-point in the sky, brightly lighting up every speck of the area below us. We had successfully avoided other hikers and campers on our trek, even though we passed a few groups of lean-tos and yurts. The app wasn't wrong when it said this area is popular with backcountry hikers and campers. I hope they are all safe.

The hike itself had been a slog. Roots clawed across the path like tripwires, mud tried to steal my boots, and the air smelled perpetually of damp pine needles and old granite. Honestly, it was beautiful. Black-capped chickadees fluttered overhead, scolding us for intruding. Every time my foot slipped, Bo would offer unhelpful advice like "Balance, wizard" or "Try using your legs properly." By the time we reached the cliffs, my calves were burning, my shirt clung to me with sweat, and my hiking app cheerfully told me I'd burned enough calories to justify three donuts. Bo insisted that meant six.

"Back to the pretzel lady now?" Bo asked, staring down at the glacial basin before us.

"What? Why would you even think that's a possibility?" We had passed a campsite with a few twenty-somethings enjoying some Maine-grown herbs, and they had snacks for Bo. He had graciously accepted. I've never seen him say no to a good snack.

"You don't buy pretzels. I like pretzels."

"I'll add it to the shopping list," I replied. "Can we stay focused, please? Maybe that dragon vision of yours can see more than I'm able to."

Bo let out a little woof and lifted his leg on a tuft of grass growing between the rocks.

"Nothing special. Just forest stuff. I wish I saw a food truck. Tacos would be good right now"

"Let's try this," I suggested, pulling the Amulet of Illumination from my shirt and lifting it to my right eye. For years, I thought the necklace my grandfather gave me was just a cool old piece of jewelry. Only a chance wardrobe slip, witnessed by the Protectors while they were having lunch, allowed us to discover what it really was. The pendant hangs around my neck on a simple gold chain. There is hardly a day when I don't wear it.

I was working and had bent over to pick up a few coasters that had fallen when I was serving lunch to the guys. The amulet slipped out of my shirt, and the Protectors had a minor freak-out. Red told me that day, "The Amulet of Illumination allows a user to see hidden objects, regardless of the magic they are concealed by. That includes a dragon in hiding."

That pendant wasn't just some shiny old knick-knack. It was, apparently, one of the rarest dragon treasures of all time. The Protectors said there were only a handful of them in the last thousand years, which basically meant I had been walking around with a world-class magical artifact in my pocket, thinking it was just cool-looking costume jewelry. I remembered turning it over in my hands, running my thumb across the grooves. Warm to the touch when it should've been cold. Hypnotic patterns that made me feel like I was about two seconds away from falling into some kind of trance. The thing could reveal anything hidden, no matter the spell, including dragons in disguise. You can imagine how thrilled Bo must've been to hear that part.

Then came the kicker. According to Jim, that crystal in the middle wasn't just some fancy rock. It was infused with the dying essence of an ancient dragon. Apparently, when one of the oldest and most powerful dragons was killed in a crystal cavern, it dumped its last breath of magic into the nearest shiny gem. Lucky me, right? The dragonslayer who found it thought, "Hey, why not make jewelry out of this?" and the crystal was split into three pieces, each one carved into an eye-shaped amulet. The carvings weren't for show. They trapped the dragon's essence inside. I always respect the power of the ancient magical artifacts. To do otherwise would be a huge mistake.

"Do you see anything?" Bo asked. "Flying moose men anywhere to be found?"

"There are glowing trails across the sky," I said. "They're kind of like when an airplane flies overhead and leaves a contrail. But I can only see these with the amulet. Something powerful left a mark on the sky when it passed overhead. Up here, that can only mean one thing."

We needed to move around. "Let's try a different perspective. The trail heads down towards the pond."

"Flying is faster."

I gave that serious consideration for a few seconds. Bo was right. Now that we're here, we can cover a lot more ground in our search without worrying about a trick storm taking us out of commission. Some low-level flight within the Chimney Pond basin might be a good plan.

"I think you're right, Bo. A little dragon and rider activity might even draw a Thunderbird out into the open for a little tete-a-tete."

He didn't hesitate.

Bo's transformation is always both awe-inspiring and frightening at the same time. How something so small can become such a large and powerful being is nothing short of incredible. The process is a dramatic tearing away of illusion to reveal the ancient power that lies hidden just beneath the surface. Or in this case, just beneath the fur.

The transformation from a squat, snub-nosed, drooling mess to a mighty dragon begins with a low growl that is more like the rumble of not-so-distant thunder. Bo's brown eyes flicker and change, flashing with a gold-flecked molten glow. The air around him shimmers as his body begins to stretch and grow. Shadows appear even in the brightest daylight. Magic has a way of shifting the laws of the universe.

At first, his limbs begin to lengthen, stretching and popping quickly into a new shape. The brown fur vanishes, melting into shimmering, iridescent scales that represent every shade of red in a box of Crayola crayons and a dozen more, with a mix of bronze and burnished gold. His body grows rapidly, expanding to the size of a city garbage truck. His back arches, allowing a spine of armored plating to emerge. That is followed by the massive wings unfurling from his flanks, mighty, leathery, and each the size of a sail. His stumpy bulldog tail twitches and grows, lengthening like a whip into something more serpentine and powerful, flicking back and forth with power and control.

The air filled with ozone, hot and metallic, carrying the scent of stone scorched by dragon fire. Standing so close to him during the shift always left my skin tingling, as though the universe itself brushed a static charge over me. It wasn't just a physical change, it was reality reasserting itself, reminding me that dragons were not supposed to be hidden in bulldog disguises. They were supposed to rule the skies.

In front, his snout elongates, smoke flows from his nostrils, and his lips pull back to reveal a massive and powerful set of gleaming white teeth that would make any dentist proud. In less than 30 seconds, Bocephus has gone from a goofy little French Bulldog to a creature from a storybook. A true dragon, ancient and elemental. But even more importantly, my best friend.

No matter how many times I see it, part of me still expects him to shake himself off afterward like a wet dog. Instead, I get muscle, fire, and wings big enough to blot out half the sky. It makes me feel small in the best way, like standing in front of the ocean or under a cathedral dome. You can't help but believe in something bigger than yourself. And yet, when his eye flicks back to me, golden and sharp, I know he's waiting, not for orders, but for partnership. That's the difference. He's not just a dragon, and I'm not just a wizard. We're something else entirely, and the world has no name for it yet.

"What are you waiting for?" he said smugly, twisting his neck down to look at me. "Let's go. Cue the heroic soundtrack. "

"Enough with the catchphrases."

I stepped forward, climbing up onto Bo's back. The granite cliffs loomed over us, sharp and watching. The pond shimmered below like a perfect mirror. I placed my hands on the familiar spikes protruding from his neck and braced myself.

"Let's ride the sky," I whispered.

"And some there be that have no fear of dragons, for they sleep deep in the bones of mountains, and the mountains sleep in them."

John Gardner, Grendel

CHAPTER ELEVEN

THE LEGEND IS CLEAR

We flew above the landscape, watching the impossibly rich hues of autumn whiz below us. I've become more comfortable as a dragon rider, so I'm less white-knuckled as we fly than I used to be. The air at this elevation was crisp and cool, leaving me wishing for my long coat. It wasn't exactly made for hiking, so I had to forego that. I did remember to bring my goggles, so at least I was able to see where we were going.

Below us, the forest rippled like a living carpet, branches swaying in the wind like waves on the sea. The scent of pitch and damp earth rose even this high up, carried on the cold breath that rolled off the mountain. Bo's wingbeats thudded like distant drums, steady and unrelenting, each downward sweep filling my chest with vibration. My nerves were tight, strung like a bowstring, but I forced myself to breathe through it. It was almost peaceful, until it wasn't.

The eagle-like creature appeared out of nowhere next to us. Even Bo was caught by surprise, his head twisting to get a better look.

The thing didn't just appear. It manifested. One moment, there was only sky and rolling clouds. The next a shimmer bent the air like heat on asphalt, and out of it came wings. Massive, feathered, their span so broad they blotted out a swath of sun. The figure's body was half-hidden in the glare, human-shaped but too large, and then the antlers broke through the light, silhouetted against the sky. My stomach dropped.

"Bo, is this some kind of altitude sickness or hallucination caused by over-exertion and hunger?"

"I see it, too."

"It looks like a flying man, but with wings as large as an eagle."

"And a moose head," Bo corrected. "Not just a man."

I knew the legends were true in that instant.

"Pamola," I said out loud.

The voice we heard next was unexpectedly friendly. Masculine, but non-threatening.

"Why have you come to my mountain? I will allow you time to respond."

The words didn't pass through my ears the way typical sound did. They settled into my bones, into the hollows of my chest. It wasn't thunder, not yet, but it had that same presence, the way a storm rolls in and fills the air before rain even falls. Bo's wings faltered once, just a fraction, betraying the fact that even a dragon could feel the weight of that voice.

"Well, we ..." I began to stammer.

The smooth voice went on, "Most do not receive this courtesy. You are special, and your companion is unlike any other we have seen for centuries."

Think fast, Wilder. I really should have been more prepared for this moment. Fortunately for me, I gained a few extra seconds when Bo's voice thundered across the sky, bold and emphatic.

"I am ... Dragon. Do ...not ... interfere."

Wow, that's a powerful message. I hope my dragon buddy can back it up.

Bo spoke only to me after I had that thought. "Must be strong. They will respect that."

We flew in silence, the water now flashing below us in the sunshine, a glacial pond so pristine that swimming isn't even allowed.

My goggles caught the reflection of wings across that water—his, ours, overlapping until I couldn't tell which belonged to which. The silence pressed heavily, thicker than the thin alpine air. My heart thudded against my ribs in time with Bo's wingbeats. This wasn't like the Kiwakwa, or even Draco Marinus. This wasn't a creature. This was... a presence.

"I am Pamola, and the Thunderbirds have protected this mountain for eternity." The voice was friendly but unmistakably used to being in charge and or worshipped.

"Why do you bring your magic here?"

"Bo, he knows who and what we are! How can he know that?"

I spoke to the eagle moose man flying alongside us, "We came for your help, oh great one."

I heard and felt Bo sigh, "You sound weak. Be strong."

"Follow." Simple and direct. Pamola veered toward the highest cliff face.

Since this area is so popular with campers and hikers, I had to assume this legendary Thunderbird is as magical and skilled as Bo in the art of not being seen. Was it actually the embodiment of the Penobscot legends, though?

Bo followed without hesitation, his body tilting into the draft as Pamola cut ahead like a blade through silk. I clung tight, the cold air slicing my cheeks raw, every nerve in me screaming that this was the kind of invitation you didn't refuse. The mountain loomed closer, cliffs like jagged teeth, shadows pooling in their crevices.

He led us to a craggy cliff face with a flat area wide enough for Bo to come to rest. The three of us stood on that wide rocky ledge, two thousand feet above the pond and wooded basin.

Wind howled across the ledge, tugging at my clothes, tearing at my hair. The stone beneath my boots was slick from centuries of storms. Bo crouched, wings folding tight, his heat radiating against my back as if to shield me. Pamola descended without effort, wings folding with the elegance of a falcon stooping.

"I ask for the final time. Why are you here?"

It could be a trick of the imagination, but he seemed smaller in stature here on the side of the mountain. Pamola still looked like a man with the head of a moose and eagle wings folded and tucked neatly behind his back, but here he was only a foot taller than me. His mouth didn't move when he spoke, but the words were clear as a bell. So was the implication of not answering.

"We have come to seek your help. People are disappearing."

"Transgressors must be removed," he replied gently, almost making it sound like a favor. "The land is mine to protect."

I needed a little clarification. I also needed to have my head examined. I'm just a waiter, not a magical diplomat. I wish the other Protectors could have come with me, they have centuries more experience. Speaking to a moose would be off-putting enough. Standing in front of a legendary moose-man-eagle is even worse.

Bo spoke up instead. "Why did you awaken?"

Bo's question surprised me a little, but Pamola didn't seem to think it was odd that a giant red dragon was talking to him on this little mountain-top rest area.

"What do you mean ... awaken?" I asked.

The Thunderbird responded, turning away from Bo to face me.

"I have slumbered for a long time. The time of the Thunderbirds passed, and I slept here on this mountain-top, hidden deep in this cave. I awaited my time to return when the mountain needed me, unknown and undetected as the world changed around it. Recently, something caused me to awaken. A new energy is flowing into our world."

Pamola's wings shivered once as he said it, and the gust nearly knocked me backward. I steadied myself, skin prickling. New energy. The phrase echoed, full of weight. Did he mean Bo's arrival? Or was there something more going on?

"Are you the one responsible for the five people who have vanished recently? You can't just grab people ..."

I was interrupted sternly this time. Pamola's voice was ever so slightly louder and more insistent.

"I protect the mountain. I am the spirit of the wind and storm. I bring the lightning and prevent harm to the land."

"So ... you're saying yes."

"Those that I removed sought to change the land. Their minds were clear with intention: to cut down the trees, to dig into the earth and plunder her riches, to drain the water from the lakes and waterways. I will not allow this to happen."

"They were just hikers passing through!"

I placed my hand on my belt buckle, prepared to whip it off my waist and transform it into a sword if we were threatened. My belt is where I conceal my grandfather's legendary sword, and so far, I haven't had to whip it out. St. George the Dragonslayer left me this sword, and for a few years it languished in my closet. The concealment spell was so powerful that it took a dragon to reveal it to me. Ever since then, I've kept it around my waist, concealed under a new spell. It's more convenient than carrying around a walking stick or umbrella, and nobody would ever suspect a simple leather belt would be the sword of legend.

Pamola's tone became less friendly and more impatient, his voice deeper and more bombastic. "They were much more than that. They came to this land with ill intentions. Greed drove them. Others were simple, and I removed them for leaving their filth and waste behind."

Pamola paused and looked at me, then Bo. The moose head turned downwards and looked directly at my waist, where my hand rested on the belt buckle.

"Hold on," I needed clarification. "You killed someone for littering?"

"My role is clear, and the mountain is sacred. You must leave now. I have only spoken to you because the small ones asked me to do so."

"Small ones?"

Before I could say anything else, I felt the thunder. No, the pre-thunder. The suction before lightning. A gut-twisting pressure that hit my ears and stomach before the first flash. The lightning bolt flashed merely inches from the ledge where we stood. My hair stood on end from the electricity, and my entire body vibrated from the hum it produced.

"Go now, your weapon does not frighten me," he said, turning away.

The world went white-blue, seared into my vision, the air ripped apart in a jagged crack that drowned even Bo's growl. My teeth rattled in my skull, every hair on my arms lifting. For one endless second, I felt inside the lightning, part of it, my heart faltering under the sheer force. Then it was gone, leaving ozone and smoke curling in the thin air.

Chapter Twelve

Not Dead Yet

We were back at the trailhead. Not dead, not covered with horrible burns or the fillings popped out of my teeth from being struck by lightning. Nobody had moved a muscle, but somehow Pamola had dismissed us with magic powerful enough to transport us miles away, back where we had started. That could only mean one thing: he knew we were here all along.

The shift was so sudden it left me queasy, like stepping off a carnival ride. One second, we were on a mountain ledge facing a god. Next, my boots were crunching gravel at the trailhead, the truck parked neatly in front of us as though nothing had happened. The sun hadn't even shifted much. My stomach pitched, my head spun, and I had to remind myself to breathe.

Bo switched back to being a dog again. Nonplussed, he only had one thought.

"Lunchtime?"

"Are you kidding me? We just had a meeting with a literal deity, the thunder god and protector of the mountain, and all you can think about is lunch?"

"Always thinking about lunch."

We hopped into Red's truck and headed back toward town. It was time for lunch.

The road unspooled in front of us, pines and birches lining both sides like silent witnesses. My knuckles were white on the wheel, the adrenaline still fizzing in my bloodstream. Bo, meanwhile, sat shotgun with his chin propped on the window, watching trees whip by with the utter serenity of someone who a thunder god hadn't just dismissed. Every now and then his tail thumped against the seat, probably imagining the pancakes he'd order.

When we arrived at the same restaurant we had breakfast earlier, the waitress looked at us as she tucked a pencil behind her ear and said, "Back again, I see. You two having an okay day? You look like you've been through the wringer."

"It's been an interesting morning," I responded drily. Bo let out a low woof.

"Sit down wherever you like. My name's Rhonda, I'll get you a cup of coffee and a bowl of water for the little pooch."

She dropped those off along with a menu and said she'd be "back in a flash" to take our orders. She didn't even bat an overly long fake eyelash at Bo sitting in the chair across from me in the booth.

That was the thing about small-town diners. Nobody cared what you looked like when you came through the door, whether you had leaves and pine needles in your hair, or a dog sitting upright like a paying customer. Places like this survived on routine, gossip, and strong coffee, not judgment. Still, I tugged my sleeves down, trying to hide the faint tremble in my hands.

"Can we take a minute to review?" I said to Bo as I scanned the menu. I was careful to keep my voice low so none of the other diners would hear me, even though only four of the two dozen tables were currently occupied. I had also taken a table with my back to everyone, so they were less likely to see my lips moving.

"The moose eagle man is real, that's the top of the list of Important Things To Remember."

"And powerful," Bo added, in my head but not out loud. "Very powerful.' Bo doesn't have an indoor voice, so he's become more careful about talking in public.

"Right, powerful enough to send us packing without any noticeable effort. God-like status confirmed. We read up a bit on Pamola, the Thunderbird legends, and other Penobscot stories. I've got to admit, talking to a being with the head of a moose, the body of a man, and the wings and feet of an eagle was a lot easier than I would have predicted."

"More pancakes."

"What? Yes, of course. Sorry for being focused on the extremely alarming situation of a legendary god killing passersby while you want to have another stack of pancakes."

"Blueberry sounds good. I'm hungry."

"You are irrepressible."

"I'm a dragon. I get hungry. Doesn't mean I'm not listening."

His eyes glimmered faintly gold at that, a reminder that beneath the stumpy snout and drooly jowls was a predator older than most civilizations. Dragons could hold two truths at once: hunger and focus. Or at least, Bo could.

"Right, sorry. I know you're as committed to this as I am. What do we do next, though?"

We paused our conversation when Rhonda came back to take our order. I asked for the meatloaf special, since I love mashed potatoes. She smiled, pulled the pencil from behind her ear, and wordlessly wrote down Bo's order when I asked for a stack of blueberry pancakes for the dog, as if it were something she heard every day. Who knows, maybe she does? After she walked away, Bo answered my question.

"Get help. We need help. And extra syrup."

The phrase landed heavier than I expected. Bo rarely admitted to needing outside aid. His dragon pride usually stopped him long before that. But he was right. Pamola wasn't just another adversary. He was a force of nature with antlers. You didn't fight that alone.

The rest of the meal was uneventful, thankfully. We headed back to Red's truck for the drive south. We talked for a long time on the three-and-a-half-hour ride home. We both agreed the help we need isn't something Red and John Patrick can provide. Although they are very well-versed in the American Indian legends surrounding Mt. Katahdin, Pamola, and the

Thunderbirds, we need more in-depth insight if we're going to be effective in our talks with the actual ancient god. I still can't believe that's what we're dealing with, but the evidence is overwhelming.

"Hey, remember when Pamola said something about the small ones?"

"Tiny moose men?"

"No, I think he meant the Mikumwess. They are the small ones of Indian legend."

"And you know them."

"I do. When we get back home, we're going to pay them a visit. I haven't talked to them in over a decade, but this seems like the right time to rekindle an old friendship."

"After lunch."

"Of course, God forbid you might have to skip a meal," I responded sarcastically.

Bo just wagged his tail against the vinyl seat, entirely un-bothered. Outside the truck windows, the Maine woods streamed past. The forests were old, secretive, and patient. Somewhere in those shadows, the Mikumwess were waiting, and I had a feeling they'd been expecting me for longer than I realized.

Chapter Thirteen

OLD FRIENDS

I visit my grandmother regularly. She always fixes a good meal, and we talk about all the regular things. Work, her favorite TV shows, and when I'll finally ask Valerie to marry me so we can settle down and have kids.

"Grandma, we've only been dating a few months. Slow down."

She always laughs and says, "You're not getting any younger, you know."

Her laugh always reminds me of summer porches and iced tea, the kind of sound that makes you feel instantly younger. The clink of her spoon in a teacup, the faint smell of whatever she's baking, those things are more magical to me than any spell I've learned from Red or John Patrick. If the world ever tipped completely sideways, I know her kitchen could set it right again.

This time, however, I didn't want to stop and visit. Bo and I needed to quietly pass through her yard to the trail leading into the woods. That's the way to the Mikumwess. I had more than a few encounters with them growing up, but it's been a decade since I walked through these woods. The Mikumwess are the Native American spirits of the forest and are small and wise in the ways of nature. I always enjoyed my conversations with them as a youth. They taught me to accept my growing powers as a gift.

We walked the mile from my apartment to Grandma's house and cut down her side yard along the row of hedges. This time of day, she's usually napping in front of The Price Is Right on TV, so the likelihood of her looking out the window was low.

As we entered the woods in the back of the yard, I heard the familiar sound of her screen door opening.

"You boys stop in when you're done with whatever you're doing out there. I'll bake some brownies."

I turned, caught in the act. Grandma waved, her face bright with mischief.

Her wave carried that same unshakable certainty she always had, as if she knew exactly where I was going and why, even if I hadn't told her. For all I knew, maybe she did. Grandma's eyes have a way of seeing more than most.

I smiled back. How does she always know?

"Okay, Grandma!"

Bo woofed softly, his stubby tail wagging.

The scent of the apple trees in the back corner of the yard followed us as we stepped beneath the first line of pines, a boundary I'd always thought of as a gate. Behind us was the ordinary world of brick houses and sidewalks; before us was the deep, timeless hush of the forest. Even as a kid, I'd felt the shift here, like stepping through a portal.

The forest sounds took over quickly as we worked our way down the path. Squirrels and chipmunks crisscrossed the forest floor in search of their next meal, birds hopped from branch to branch overhead, and the noise from the world faded away into a natural silence that most people don't ever get to enjoy. Despite the crunchy leaves underfoot, the silence wrapped around us like a blanket.

It only took a few minutes before I heard the first laughter from behind a tree trunk. Another laugh from a different direction quickly matched it. They were with us already.

Spotting a fallen tree just off the path, I veered toward it and took a seat. Bo plopped down by my side, and we waited.

"It has been a long time, Wilder Blackwood. We wondered when you would visit us again."

A figure emerged from behind a spruce, a familiar face from my childhood. Barely four feet tall, with brown skin, black hair, and a white beard that reached his chest. Animal skins covered his middle, but his eyes were sharp as stars. Three more Mikumwess flanked him. When he spoke, it was in a language I did not understand with my ears, but easily understood in my head.

The sight of him pulled me back instantly to childhood — to a time when I'd sat cross-legged in this same clearing, being taught how to coax sparks into flame or how to listen to the "voice" of water in a brook. They hadn't changed a bit, except maybe to look even smaller, more delicate, against the taller trees. Yet the aura they carried of ageless patience, humor, and authority all at once was precisely the same.

"And you are Bocephus, the mighty dragon. Welcome."

Bo woofed in return as the Mikumwess leader scratched him on top of his head.

"How do you know?" I asked.

"This is our land. We are the spirits of the forest. We know all who enter."

Of course they did. I don't know where they live, if they have a secret village in the woods, or how they spend their daily lives. I just know that whenever I needed guidance, I only had to walk into the woods and they would find me.

"It's been a long time, but I need your help," I said. They were all eye-level with me since I was sitting on the log.

"Yes," he replied with a smile. "We told Pamola to be kind to you."

We were right! "How did you know we were in Katahdin?"

All of the Mikumwess surrounding us laughed, their voices mixing with the susurration of the blowing leaves in the tree-tops above us to sound completely natural.

"We are Mikumwess. This is our home, and that is our home. All of the forest is our home."

The laughter wasn't mocking. It was light and contagious, like the sound of cousins giggling around a fire. There was a comfort in it, a reminder that magic wasn't always sharp edges and storm clouds. Sometimes it was just joy.

I owed them a debt of gratitude. They studied me. My childhood teachers of magic now seemed smaller, older, yet somehow greater.

"Thank you for watching out for us. That situation could have turned out quite differently if you hadn't warned Pamola of our arrival," I said.

"He knew you were there. We only asked for respect and fair treatment. Sometimes he reacts first and asks questions later."

I had so many questions, I didn't know which to ask first. As an adult, I have different feelings regarding my power. So much has changed since I met Red and John Patrick. And Jim, of course. I am a Protector now, much like Pamola is the protector of the mountain.

The Mikumwess leader spoke again, "You have changed much since you last visited us. The child is now a man, and a special and powerful man. You have taken good care of the people who need you."

Reaching out to Bo without leaning down, he placed his palm on top of Bo's head.

"We have never met one of your kind or even known of your existence. You are fascinating to us. Even Pamola would be wise to be respectful."

Bo's golden eyes flickered faintly at that, pride swelling in him like heat rising off stone. Still, he stayed quiet, letting the moment belong to them. For once, my dragon wasn't cracking jokes. He was absorbing their words, and maybe even enjoying the rare honor of being petted like a common house dog by ancient spirits.

Interesting, I thought. Is Bocephus, the Earth Dragon, as mighty as a Thunderbird? Pamola is said to be the elemental spirit of storm and wind, punishing those who trespass on Mount Katahdin. Dragons are also elemental creatures, often protecting a sacred place or item of their own. In Eastern traditions, dragons are often regarded as wise and spiritual beings, frequently viewed as closer to gods than mere creatures. There are more similarities than I ever considered.

Bo had been quiet this entire visit, soaking it all in. His voice came into my head, "This is your place, and these are your people. I am only a guest."

The other Mikumwess slowly stepped up to Bocephus. Some patted him on the head, others scratched him behind the ears. He reveled in the attention like any dog would. The

Mikumwess, however, could feel the dragon beneath the surface. This was entirely new for them, and they were loving it. Bo was making a lot of new friends today.

"Please don't roll over for belly scratches," I admonished.

The leader continued to explain, "For Pamola to trust you, you must prove yourself. Only then will he accept you completely. When he sees you as a trustworthy guardian of the land, he will have faith in your words that the trespassers are nidabe. Friend."

I needed to ensure the safety of hikers and campers in Baxter State Park surrounding Mouth Katahdin. What kind of test would an ancient Wabanaki deity deem acceptable in order to trust me?

"Okay," I said. "I'm in. What do I need to do?"

He smiled and rested his hand on my shoulder, as heavy as a stone.

"I knew you would not shrink from the task. You are indeed a great Protector of man. You must walk the Trial of the Hidden Path. It is a challenge, designed from your youth, and not to be taken lightly."

The other Mikumwess hummed softly, almost like wind moving through reeds, as if the very trees approved of this decision. The air thickened with expectation, and I knew there was no turning back. The Hidden Path wasn't just a trial. It was a bridge between who I had been as a boy and who I was now becoming.

Chapter Fourteen

THE HIDDEN PATH

The Mikumwess leader lifted his hand and pointed toward the arch of pine boughs ahead. "There," he said. "The Hidden Path begins. What you face within is not of us, but of yourself. Walk, and be judged." His eyes glimmered with warmth but also weight, as though he already knew what waited for me inside. Bo snorted, but even he grew quiet at the gravity in the little spirit's tone.

The Mikumwess didn't do an outstanding job explaining what the "Trial of the Hidden Path" is, exactly. A test, and no more explanation than that. I assume a test of strength and power, so Bo and I were ready to begin.

My phone dinged with a text. "Hey, Wilder. Can you work a double tomorrow? Two people called out sick already." It was from Parker, my boss at Red's Riverside Tavern.

No problem. First, I have to finish a test from Maine forest elves in order not to get into a fight with a mountain eagle moose man. A double shift is not a big deal. Instead, I replied, "You got it, boss!" and tucked the phone back into my front pocket.

Five Mikumwess stood in line next to a pine bough entrance in the forest. Their eyes glinted like the embers of a slow-burning campfire. The branches overlapped each other, leaving a small doorway for us to stoop through to the darkened path beyond.

Bo finally spoke up, "This is like when Yoda sent Luke Skywalker into that scary cave in Return of the Jedi."

"It was Empire Strikes Back, and it's nothing like that," I whispered back at him.

"Just the same," Bo retorted. "You need a light saber."

I had the next best thing around my waist. Or maybe even better.

I unbuckled the belt and felt the magic shift. I whipped it in front of me, willing the enchantment away. Instead, my hand now gripped the sword of my grandfather, a centuries-old weapon filled with its own magic.

"You will not need that," one of the Mikumwess said.

"Well … uh … " I stammered hesitantly. "Just in case I need to clear a path, I'll keep it ready."

We stepped through the pine archway.

The sun didn't fade, the forest didn't go silent. In fact, there was nothing different on this side from the other side. No change at all. The only reason the path looked darker from the other side was that a giant pine tree cast a shadow to our right.

The trail dropped off a hundred feet later, swerving a hard left down the side of a mountain. I practically grew up playing in these woods, and there is not a mountain here. The test has begun. Bo didn't have much trouble navigating the large rocks that blocked the packed-dirt path, but I had to keep one eye ahead of me and one eye on the ground so I wouldn't trip up. The sun-dappled trail was easy to see but difficult to maneuver. I quickly realized that descending with the sword in my hand was potentially dangerous to my own well-being. Renewing the concealment spell, I tucked the belt into the loops around my waist, buckled it up, and kept moving.

The forest had grown unfamiliar in an instant. Each rock seemed sharper, each patch of moss slicker. The air itself pressed heavier, thick with the scent of pine pitch and wet leaves. Sweat dripped from my temples, sliding past my jaw as if even my body understood this was no ordinary walk in the woods. The silence between birdsong felt too long, like the animals were holding their breath to see if I'd fall.

Rocks jutted from the dirt, slick with moss. Branches whipped across my arms. Sweat ran down my back. Hours blurred together. The descent got even steeper and more perilous, the way blocked by broken branches every dozen feet. At more than one spot, I had to pick up the dog and carry him over the deadfall. Bo didn't like that very much, and the compact bulldog weight strained my back and legs as we moved through the woods.

At one point, I slipped on a patch of loose shale and slid a good ten feet, bark shredding my palms as I grabbed at a sapling to stop. Bo barked sharply, half warning, half annoyance, and it echoed back as if the forest itself mocked me. My thighs burned, my shoulders ached, and still the trail plunged downward, like it had no intention of letting us turn back. Where did this mountain come from?

The slope finally evened out as we reached the bottom of the incline hours later. Without warning, both of my feet sank into the thick, oozing muck. Bo was more fortunate. He had been relieving himself on a tree when the ground changed under me, and he was on more solid footing at the base of the tall white pine.

My boots had plunged to the ankle in muck. Then to the shin. Then deeper. The stink of rot filled my nose. Panic rose like floodwater. I yanked upward, but the mud sucked tighter, gripping like claws.

"Bo, I can't move! My feet are stuck in this mud. Why didn't I see it before I stepped into it?"

Bo shook his head, bulldog jowls flopping, "Maybe it wasn't there."

I strained against the suction that was created every time I tried to lift a foot out of the brown and green sludge. I fought against the pull as my heart hammered in my chest. I didn't want to lose a boot; these Timberlands aren't cheap. I could feel the laces loosening with each tug, and I could tell my left boot was almost off my foot already. I felt a tingle of magic moving through my body, but I suppressed it. I need to do this on my own. I may be a 28-year-old waiter living in a small town, but I don't need magic to get myself out of every little predicament.

"Hey, Bo. Any ideas?" I asked, panic rising in my voice.

"Lay down," came the simple response. I swear he was enjoying this moment a little.

"Lay down? That's exactly what I'm not ..." and then I remembered something I learned a long time ago. I gently lay on my back, the thick mud supporting me without sinking. Now that my weight was spread out across a larger area, I could feel the mud's grip on my feet loosen. Slowly, agonizingly, I wriggled backward. My feet popped free with a sickening *slurp*. Wiggling my legs and lifting them at the same time, they popped to the surface with surprisingly less effort than I expected.

"I wish I had remembered that earlier!" I exclaimed, both to Bo and to myself. I rolled to the side, keeping my weight spread out on the mud. After a few rolls, I was at the base of Bo's tree and able to sit up on my knees. I thought I saw a huge, winged shadow pass overhead as thunder rumbled in the distance, but when I looked up, nothing was visible. A trick of the light, the play of sun and clouds on my eyes.

The mud clung to me in thick ropes, stinking of rot and stagnant water. I scraped it from my boots with a stick, but the smell followed me. My skin crawled as if the earth itself had tried to claim me, a reminder that this test wasn't about fighting monsters, it was about surviving the things that swallowed you slowly.

"I need to rest for a minute before we keep moving," I said as I huffed and puffed.

"Maybe a gym membership when we get back," he grinned that bulldog grin.

I looked directly into Bo's brown eyes, now showing a little golden dragon twinkle.

"Now isn't the time. We've got a challenge to find. I don't even know what we're looking for."

I reached up and snapped a dead branch off the pine. It was as thick as my wrist and eight feet long. It would be a solid walking stick and valuable to test the ground in front of us as we progressed. The trail we started on had withered away to nothing. Our direction wasn't clear, and neither of us was confident about the direction we were headed in, but we walked. Hours passed, and nothing looked any different. The woods around us never changed, and no challenge presented itself. I was beginning to feel like a failure. A hungry and thirsty failure.

The sameness of the forest became its own enemy. Every tree mirrored the last, every stretch of moss the same sickly green. My throat dried, my tongue thick with the taste of rot from the mud. Bo padded beside me in silence, his ears flicking at sounds I couldn't hear. Now and then the wind whispered like laughter, but when I stopped, the woods stood mute, waiting.

"Bo, it's late and getting dark. Do you think we should stop for the night so we don't get more lost?"

He looked around and woofed.

"Hungry. Good berries over there," he said as he sniffed the air.

My stomach growled so loudly it echoed in the trees. I chewed a few sour red berries, bitter enough to make me gag.

Bo laughed, dropped to the ground, and curled up as much as his chubby little body would allow. He was snoring within seconds.

I broke off a few thick pine boughs from nearby trees to use as protection from the elements. Closer to Bo, I pushed some leaves into a pile next to him. The dry leaves would serve as my mattress, and the layers of pine branches provided a natural blanket to help trap some of my body heat. Exhausted, sleep came like drowning.

Dreams came fast and strange. I saw myself still in the mud, but this time the muck rose up and formed into hands, pulling me under. Above, thunder rumbled, but it wasn't a storm. It was laughter, deep and knowing. I woke with a start, breath fogging the cool predawn air, my body stiff from the makeshift bed.

Sleep was elusive for the next few hours. I woke up just after dawn and heard the angry buzzing around my head. The first sting on my neck was a warning shot and a nasty alarm clock. I slapped at it and asked Bo, "Do dogs get stung by mosquitoes?"

"Yes, very annoying," he answered even more gruffly than usual. He even let out a bark before he stopped to scratch at his ear with his back leg.

One mosquito turned into ten, and ten quickly became a hundred. I was smacking and slapping every exposed area of my body and some that weren't exposed. Bo dropped and rolled around on the ground, trying to create a dirt barrier on his body. Mosquitos and black flies are the bane of any hiker in the Maine woods, and we had just wandered into a swarm of them. The bugs were so thick that the air became shadowy as it filled with them. More and more of the tiny beasts arrived, drawn to the heat of our bodies and the carbon dioxide we both exhaled as we tried to run through the woods. What I wouldn't give for a can of mosquito repellent right now.

They bit everything. My arms. My neck. My eyelids. I slapped and clawed, smearing blood and welts across my skin. The sound of their whining filled my skull.

Bo rolled in dirt, whimpering. His jowls flapped as he snapped at them.

"Zap them!" he barked, with a tone of frustration in his voice. The smoke began to curl from his nostrils.

"No flames!" I shouted. "This entire area could go up in a flash."

A sudden gust of wind blew across the forest floor. Dry leaves lifted off the ground and spiraled in the air, the pine needles from a dozen years of needle drop swirled around our feet, and every single mosquito just ... blew away.

We stood silent for a moment, then Bo burst out laughing.

"That was easy!"

"I wouldn't call it easy," I said, looking around. "But I would call it convenient."

The woods grew quiet again, but my nerves trembled.

We pressed deeper.

Even in their absence, I felt the bugs crawling on me. Welts burned across my arms, and my skin itched like fire. Each step became a choice: scratch and stumble, or grit my teeth and endure. Bo looked miserable, too. His eyes narrowed, dirt still clinging to his fur. Yet when the wind shifted again, carrying the faintest roll of thunder, I knew it wasn't chance. Pamola was watching. Testing.

We picked what seemed like a good direction and plodded onward. For the next few hours, we discussed Valerie's sandwiches and how much we would love to eat one right now. We discussed Italian sandwiches, hot pastrami sandwiches, cold cut combos, and chicken salad sandwiches in detail. There's no sandwich shop out here in the woods, so we agreed to keep our eyes open for more wild berries growing in the area. It's months past blueberry and blackberry season, but elderberries should still be around. Too bad I never took that foraging class Valerie talked about. It would be very helpful right now.

The brush got thick, stabbing and grabbing at us as we pushed through the woods. My idea about using the sword to clear brush didn't seem too silly now, but I was determined only to use the tools the forest provided for me. In the back of my mind, it seemed necessary, given that Mikumwess had set this up, and Pamola would be the ultimate judge when I finally figured out the challenge and completed it.

The thicket appeared without warning. First one scratch across my calf. Then another, deeper, across my arm. Soon, every branch ended in thorns like daggers.

Blood welled hot and sticky. My flannel shredded.

A thorny bush snagged my pants leg and wouldn't let go. As I pulled, the thorn drove itself into my calf: Buckthorn, and a lot of it. Looking around, I could see that we were now surrounded by buckthorn, and no easy exit through it. I reached down to my injured calf and pulled out the thorn. It was almost as long as a toothpick, and only a little thicker. Buckthorn has these thorns near the tip of every branch, so it looked like a lot of pain was coming our way.

"Be careful, Bo," I cautioned. Those berries will make you sick. Another useful Boy Scout memory rising to the surface.

"I'm more concerned about you getting stabbed by a thousand tiny daggers," he laughed.

I turned to see where he had moved to, and another thorn jabbed into my hip. Even as I yelled in surprise and grabbed the branch tip embedded in my flesh, another needle-sharp buckthorn plunged into my forearm, tearing a long gash from my elbow halfway to my wrist.

"Stop moving," Bo warned. "Don't panic. Stand still and breathe."

He was right. Hasty movements caused by panic weren't going to help. I stopped moving and closed my eyes, letting my breathing become the focus through the pain in my arm. After a minute, the panic receded, and clarity returned. I slowly removed the offending forest stilettos and looked around for Bo again.

"I'm down here," he said.

"I know you're down there, you're on four legs and close to the ground."

Close to the ground. As soon as I said it, the answer was obvious. Slowly crouching down so as not to get poked again, I was quickly on my hands and knees, looking into Bo's floppy face.

"See," he said. "Better down here."

The bushes grew upward, and the three feet of space closest to the ground was almost a clear path for movement. I wasn't sure if buckthorn bushes usually grew like this or if it's particular to the North Maine Woods, but I was happy to discover the anomaly. I could feel the blood oozing from my little stab wounds, and my arm needed some attention right away. My clothes were already shredded from the thorns tearing at them, and my shirt was the worst of all. Flaps of the red and black-checked material hung from me, the sleeves missing large pieces that must be snagged on branches behind us.

"This was my favorite flannel shirt," I complained.

"Stop whining. Better than your skin."

True enough, I considered. I grabbed a section of shirt on my chest and pulled. I was able to rip off a large piece of material to wrap around my arm and stop the bleeding. Now all I needed to worry about was infection. That seemed like a tomorrow problem.

Every shuffle forward left another drop of blood on the ground.

Ten minutes of crawling later, and the buckthorn surprise ended abruptly. I still don't know how we ended up surrounded by them without noticing, but we had more pressing concerns. The light was starting to fade in the sky, and we still weren't at our destination, whatever it was.

"Bo, how can it be sunset again already? We haven't even found any wild berries to eat for lunch yet."

"Don't mention lunch,' was his only response before the big splash.

As soon as he exited from under the last thornbush, the solid ground came to an end. Bo tumbled off the bank and into the slow-moving current of the river.

"Bo! Bo, are you okay?" I was ready to leap in to save him when I realized he was still only a few feet away from me.

"You know how much I hate water," he snorted, clearing the water from his stubby nose. Our battle against Draco Marinus, the sea dragon, was probably the cause.

He heard my thought and responded, "Of course that's why."

Thankfully, the current didn't carry him away. If this had been a fast-moving river, the situation could have ended a lot differently. Bo swam a few feet to a large boulder sticking above the surface of the water, climbed up onto it, and gave himself a vigorous shake.

"Are you going to sit under that bush all day?" he asked me.

"Aren't you coming back?" I asked. "I can reach you with my walking stick. You can grab it in your mouth, and I'll pull you to shore."

"Take a look around. We need to get to the other side."

Sure enough, the path was clear. In the fading golden rays of sunlight on the other side of the river, there was an opening through the trees and underbrush, not unlike the first opening we had been sent through earlier today. It might as well be labeled FINISH LINE.

"Bo, I don't want us to get separated. We need to stay next to each other as we swim to the other side. Always stick together."

He woofed in agreement. The water was only waist-deep for me. Bo was a stronger swimmer than I expected, considering French Bulldogs usually can't swim because of their big head and short snout. Never underestimate the talents of an ancient dragon. I kept one hand extended over him for the entire crossing, ready to grab his collar in case something crazy happened, but nothing did. Now through this opening and back to searching for our challenge. The Mikumwess must be getting impatient with us by now. I hope the deal still stands.

We stood on the bank of the river as Bo shook off the water. I did the same and wrung the water out of what was left of my clothes. Expecting a trail on the other side, we stepped through the arched pine bough opening.

"There are dragons to be slain in the heart of
every man."

William Butler Yeats

Chapter Fifteen

THE CHALLENGE

The Mikumwess were waiting for us. The same little men who had ushered us into the forest on this challenge hours and hours ago were standing in the same spot I had last seen them. It seemed impossible, but we just exited through the same archway that Bo and I had first entered.

The lead Mikumwess spoke softly and reassuringly, "You know some things which seem impossible have many ways of becoming reality."

"But we have to complete the challenge you set up for us. I need to prove myself to Pamola to make his stop. We just got lost on a mountain in Maine for what seemed like days, and I never even found the challenge!"

The quiet, calm voice of the Mikumwess went on, "Not only did you find your challenge, but you also excelled at it. We, the spirits of the forest, and Pamola, guardian of the mountain, have watched you. We are pleased."

Thunder rolled across the cloudless sky.

The sound rattled through my chest, deep and resonant, though the sky overhead was a bright sheet of blue. There wasn't a cloud in sight, yet the vibration of it made the hairs on my arms lift. It wasn't just noise, it was acknowledgment. A reminder that the mountain's spirit had never taken its eyes off me.

I had no idea what he was talking about, and I'm sure it showed. Looking down at my battered, bruised, and bleeding body, I saw no injuries at all. My clothing wasn't even torn.

I flexed my hands in disbelief. Just moments ago, I'd been shredded by thorns, swollen with bug bites, mud-caked and sore. Now my skin was whole, my shirt as clean as if it had been freshly laundered. The forest had stripped me bare, then given me back to myself as if to say: nothing was ever about the body, it was about what I carried inside.

"You and your dragon have a bond beyond magic, and you relied on each other to overcome every obstacle. We used a tale from your youth to challenge you in the dangerous forest. You relied on your wits instead of magic. You have proven that you can be trusted at your word, just as you trust one another with your lives."

"I remember reading a book in middle school about a kid who was lost on Mount Katahdin. That's why all of our obstacles seemed so familiar."

Thunder rolled gently across the sky again as the Mikumwess spoke a final time.

"You endured as he did, without spell or fire. You trusted your bond. Pamola has seen your heart. When you return to the mountain, Pamola has agreed to meet you."

"He will not summon you," another of the Mikumwess added. "When you are ready, you must go to him. Choice matters as much as courage."

Their words lingered, heavy as stone. My heart thudded in my ears—not from fear, but from the weight of what it meant. Pamola had agreed to meet me. That wasn't just permission, it was an invitation. And invitations from gods were rarely gentle things.

The Mikumwess turned and walked into the forest, quickly disappearing as the branches and underbrush folded around them.

"Come on, Bo. Grandma probably made us a good lunch, and she won't ask any questions about what we've been doing out here. I don't think much time has passed, anyway."

Bo shook himself once more, water spraying from his ears, and gave me a sidelong look. "Brownies beat bug bites," he said simply. I couldn't argue.

By the time we trudged out of the woods, the sun hung low and gold over Grandma's back porch. The screen door creaked open before I even set foot in her yard.

"There you are," she said, not a question but a knowing statement. "Come wash up. Brownies are just out of the oven." Hours, not days.

Bo gave me a knowing wink and trotted ahead across the lawn, shameless, tail wagging as if nothing unusual had happened. He scratched at the door until she let him in. I followed more slowly, dragging sore muscles, my clothes somehow clean but my bones still carrying the ache of every thorn, every mosquito bite, every chilled step through the river.

The kitchen smelled of sugar and cocoa, warm and rich. Sunlight through the window made dust motes glow like tiny sparks. Grandma pulled the pan from the counter and set it in front of me.

"You look like you've been through something," she said gently. Not accusing, not prying, just stating the truth in that uncanny way of hers.

I lowered into the chair, suddenly heavy. My hands trembled as I reached for the plate she slid toward me.

She placed a square of brownie onto it without another word, then slid another to Bo, who licked the crumbs like it was the greatest gift he'd ever been given.

I stared at mine. The chocolate scent brought a lump to my throat.

Pamola's thunder still echoed faintly in my memory. The weight of the Mikumwess' trial pressed against my ribs. But here, in this kitchen, with the hum of the refrigerator and the clink of Grandma's teacup against its saucer, it all felt impossibly far away.

She reached across the table, her weathered hand covering mine. Her touch was calm and steady.

"You don't have to tell me," she said. "Just eat. The world will still be here tomorrow."

I swallowed hard, blinked back the sting in my eyes, and finally took a bite.

The brownie was warm, soft, and sweet. Human. Real.

Bo nudged my leg under the table, chocolate crumbs dotting his muzzle. He looked up with that dragon-glimmer in his eyes, and for once, he didn't say a word.

For the first time since stepping through the pine-bough arch, I let myself breathe.

The tension drained from me in slow waves. Each chew was like a tether, pulling me back into the world where people worried about grocery sales, laundry, and television shows—not storms, not spirits, not ancient trials. Grandma fussed at the stove, humming a tune I half-recognized from childhood, and the sound wrapped around me tighter than any blanket. I didn't know how long Pamola would wait for me at the mountain. I didn't know if I was ready for what came next. But in this moment, with Bo's soft snores at my feet and the taste of chocolate on my tongue, I knew I was still Wilder Blackwood. Grandson, boyfriend, Protector, wizard, and man. And for tonight, that was enough.

Chapter Sixteen

BABY YOU CAN DRIVE MY CAR

Walking back to the apartment from Grandma's house, I had an idea.

"Bo, I think I need to buy a car. We can't just keep borrowing vehicles from people whenever we need to get somewhere."

"Expensive. Flying is cheaper."

"But we can't fly everywhere we need to go. I had to borrow Red's truck to get up north to Katahdin, and even worse, Valerie has to drive whenever we go somewhere on a date. It's a little embarrassing."

"She's a good driver."

"I know she's a good driver, but maybe she would like me to drive."

"So, drive her car."

I was getting frustrated because Bo didn't understand where I was coming from. I felt a little emasculated when I always had to depend on my girlfriend for a ride somewhere. That's why I borrow Red's truck half the time. I travel a lot more than I used to before Bocephus showed up at my doorstep that day. Up until then, I walked everywhere I needed to go. My job is only a half mile away, the grocery store is only a 15-minute walk, and everything I need is right here downtown. Now, I'm thrust into a world of old dude wizards and magic spells and ancient mountain gods tossing thunderbolts at us.

We stopped at the corner, waiting for the light to change. The crosswalk sign clicked to red, glowing a stern "Don't Walk." The street was empty, not a car in sight, but I shifted my weight and waited anyway.

Bo huffed. "We could cross."

"Yeah, and we could get flattened by a drunk delivery driver."

Bo grumbled. "Hungry. Could go for pizza."

"You're always hungry," I muttered.

The crosswalk signal blinked once, then flipped to "Walk" without the button being pressed. I frowned.

"Did you do that?" I asked Bo.

He blinked up at me with a look that said, *Don't blame me for your twitchy magic.*

We stepped into the street, and as soon as our feet hit the asphalt, headlights appeared a block away. A car barreled toward the intersection, but instead of slowing gradually, its brakes screamed, tires skidding as if an invisible hand yanked them. The sedan stopped dead, the driver wide-eyed and gripping the wheel like he'd just seen a ghost.

Bo trotted across with smug satisfaction. "See? Safe."

I muttered under my breath, "Yeah, safe because some poor guy's going to need new brake pads."

The driver shook his head, rubbed his eyes, and then slowly pulled away after we'd cleared the lane. I tried not to make eye contact.

We reached the opposite sidewalk, and Bo gave me another sidelong look. "Pizza."

"Not happening."

"Then cheeseburger."

I sighed, running a hand through my hair. "You know what? Forget the car. Forget all of it. I need a new life."

Bo gave a contented grunt that sounded suspiciously like laughter.

"And none of those things come with AAA roadside assistance," I muttered. "If the world ends in the backwoods of Maine, I'd rather not explain to the Protectors that I missed the fight because I was waiting for Valerie to get out of work to give me a ride. We need to be able to travel without always having to ask for a loaner. I'm going car shopping next week."

"Me, too."

"Probably not a good idea. I'm not sure if I can take a test drive with a dog. Also, I don't trust you not to do something dumb."

"I'm not going to hump the salesperson's leg, if that's what you're worried about."

I looked at Bo and remembered the time we were in the pharmacy waiting for my allergy prescription.

"Remember when you thought it would be funny to use the store's potted plant instead of waiting to go outside?"

Bo laughed in his dog/dragon way, boisterous and loud. To anyone within earshot, it was just a little brown Frenchie suddenly barking.

"That was funny. I won't do it again."

"I had to find a different pharmacy, Bo. I'm still not allowed back in that Walgreens."

"The plant died, too."

I'm not sure if Bo's takeaway lesson was the one he should be learning. He was more concerned about the plant than me finding another pharmacy. That's the only one within walking distance of our apartment. Yet another reason why I need to find a car.

Bo yawned and stretched across the couch when we got home, clearly uninterested in my mortal concerns.

"Get an F-150," he said lazily. "Good for off-road. Big enough for dragon. Not too flashy."

"You can't fit in a truck bed, Bo. You're the size of a garbage truck when you transform."

I rubbed my temples. This was going to be a long week.

Chapter Seventeen

GETTING GROUNDED

After the events of the last few days, I didn't mind working a double shift at the restaurant. It gave me a chance to think about everything without feeling like I have to take action right away. I move too quickly sometimes, and Bo doesn't do much to discourage me unless he's busy watching a good movie on TV.

The river looked ordinary enough when I crossed the parking lot. The brackish water slipped past the high granite walls on either side, seagulls harassed a cormorant near the pedestrian bridge that crosses from Saco into Biddeford. Red's River-side Tavern sat solid and familiar atop the Saco side, brick warmed by a thin sliver of fall sun. I desperately needed an ordinary afternoon. I needed to be surrounded by familiar people and things. I needed a tray in my hands and people arguing about fries versus salad and whether the chowder was "more potato than clam today." Grounding. That's what work is for me.

Parker met me at the back door with a nod and a paper inventory sheet that had already lived a life. "Appreciate you picking up the lunch shift," he said. "Your fans miss you."

"My fans?"

"The loud blue-haired one tipped me a Ghostbuster pin last week and told me I'm a 'friend of the channel.' I don't know what that means, but I assume that's your fault," he chuckled.

"The Haunt Hunters," I said, trying not to smile too much. "They're harmless."

"Plenty of people who started out harmless ..." Parker said, scratching at the back of his neck like he was thinking about a time I didn't know. He stopped himself, tucking the thoughts of the war away again. In my effort to better understand him, I had done some research into his unit. It didn't take me long to find the newspaper article about the Iraqi informant who had turned on them, leaving his entire patrol under fire in an ambush. Three men were lost that day.

He waved the inventory sheet at the kitchen. "Soup today is haddock chowder. Clamming has been bad lately." He lowered his voice and lifted his chin, eyeballing me closely. "You look like you slept in a forest."

"I did."

He opened his mouth, closed it, and handed me an order pad. No fancy electronics for this restaurant; we are strictly old-school. And also magic-safe. "Apron. Tables three through six are yours. And your dog is welcome under the host stand if he promises not to eat the coasters again."

Bo trotted past Parker like he owned the place, nails clicking on old wood, and parked himself under the host stand with a huff. "Coasters taste like sadness and spilled beer," he informed me. "I prefer meatballs."

"Work first," I muttered quietly enough that Parker couldn't hear me as I tied my apron.

By noon, the patio had filled up nicely. The September air was bright and agreeable, except for the wind that came off the water with a little too much bite for the date on the calendar. People commented. People always comment.

"Coldest lunch I've had in September since Tom Brady came back in '09 after his knee injury," a man in a Patriots cap said to his wife, rubbing his arms. "You folks crank the AC out here?"

"It's Maine," I said, setting down his Reuben and fries. "It could snow in July." He laughed. It was the right level of dumb joke to earn me an extra dollar tip.

He laughed, but as he did, he swung his elbows wide, knocking the sandwich and fries off the edge of the table. Reflexively, I willed the plate to stop in mid-air just before it hit the ground. I grabbed it quickly, lifting it back up to the table as if I had caught it myself. Since it had been hovering out of his sightline, we were safe.

"Wow, fast reflexes. You didn't even drop a fry!"

"Lots of ping-pong in high school," I responded, walking away. The more I get used to using magic on a daily basis, the more careful I need to be.

Inside, the dining room hummed with activity and conversation. The large window facing the river was fogged at the corners due to the change in temperature outside. I wiped water rings from table five, a two-top near the door with a water view, and tried not to watch the far-off line where the river bent toward the ocean and disappeared between banks of oak and maple. Ever since we came back from Katahdin, my eyes kept going to horizons like some part of me was still measuring distance to trouble.

"Stop staring," Bo said to only me from under the host stand. "You're going to drop a plate."

"I've never dropped a plate," I said out loud, which is the kind of thing you should never say out loud in a restaurant. I busied myself with table three, and my prophecy remained true.

"Hey, Wilder!" Blue Hair waved from the doorway before the host could seat them. Haunt Hunters. All three of them, as always. Blue Hair Girl with her denim jacket covered in enamel comic book character pins, Lanky Pancake Dude in a vintage Freddy Krueger tee, and Tuxedo Shirt Guy, who had upgraded to a bow tie printed on the fabric. They'd become Saturday morning regulars, but here they were on a weekday, bright-eyed and excited like they were on a mission.

"You're going to get me fired," I said, grinning anyway. "You can't just yell my name like you're in the front row at a boy band concert."

"Ghost gang's back," Bo's voice tickled my mind. "Order pancakes."

I brought them to one of my tables and grabbed some coffees before they could even ask. "Pancakes all around?"

"You know it," Tuxedo Boy grinned, already tucking a napkin into his collar to protect his fake bowtie.

Today, their usual banter was sharper, buzzing with energy. They leaned across the table, voices dropping low but urgent.

"Wilder," Blue Hair said, eyes gleaming, "you saw it too, didn't you?"

"See what?" I asked, staying cool.

"The fog at the dock!" Lanky Pancake Dude nearly shouted, then hushed himself. "We caught it on camera. It rolled in out of nowhere and obliterated everything like someone threw a blanket over the harbor. I think there was something inside it."

"Wings," Tuxedo Boy whispered. "I swear it looked like wings. Big ones." He leaned forward toward me for emphasis and stretched his arms up and out wide, "Prehistoric big."

I laughed, "Are you new around here? Fog makes shadows. It plays tricks. That's why Maine has so many lighthouses."

"Uh-huh," Blue Hair said, unconvinced. "Funny thing is, when we looked at the footage frame by frame, we saw you and your girlfriend standing right there with Bo." She tilted her head toward Bo under the bar. "You must not have seen us. One lobsterman told us he saw 'fog like a light bulb' roll between the islands. We're uploading a teaser tonight. We tagged Bo."

"Don't tag Bo," I said. "He doesn't consent to social media." Under the host stand, Bo sneezed. The host jumped.

"We're planning a follow-up at Fort Gorges later," Lanky Pancake Dude said. "If that weird light bulb fog rolls in again and there's something in it, hopefully we'll find it. This could be our biggest video yet."

My stomach dropped. Fort Gorges. Exactly where the barrier had felt thinnest. Exactly where Bo had growled like death itself was swimming under the water.

The rest of my shift blurred. Orders, tips, small talk—but my mind kept circling back to their words. If the Hunters uploaded that fog footage, if people started really looking, it wouldn't just be ghost fans watching. It could be people Wilder Blackwood didn't want noticing.

"Eat first," I said, as I brought their first stacks. "Then haunt."

They tucked into their pancakes, talking over each other about lens choices and "moody fog vibes," and I let the sound of them become part of the restaurant noise. It helped. So did the clatter of the kitchen line and Lucy's familiar bellow of

"Two chowders, a club, and a burger with no tomato—don't you put a tomato on that burger, Hank!" Grounding.

Valerie walked in like a patch of sun. She liked to pop in for a quick hello on her break sometimes, since the deli was only a few blocks away. She had a brown paper bag in one hand and her hair scooped into a messy knot that somehow always looked intentional.

"Hi, my sweet weird waiter," she said, low and bright, and kissed me quick on the cheek, which made table two ding their forks against the water glasses because small towns are like that.

"Sandwich babe," I said, rescuing the bag. "Please tell me there's an Italian with extra olives."

"For you," she said. "And a little box of dog treats I may or may not have made myself." She leaned to peek under the host stand. "Hi, Handsome."

Bo thumped his tail and put on the face he uses to convince people he's never eaten in his life. Valerie scratched his head and looked up at me. Her eyes were soft. "You okay? You texted 'home safe' last night and then nothing."

"Chowder storm," I said. "We'll talk later?"

"Tonight," she said. "I'm closing, so I get out at eight." She twisted her eyebrows together. "It's chilly today, huh? My boss says customers were coming in for hot tea like it was November."

"Just Maine being Maine," I said, and hoped it was true.

She squeezed my hand tightly and slipped back out into the sunlight. I tucked the paper bag behind the bar where Bo couldn't easily reach it and caught Parker watching me from the service end, his expression somewhere between fond and suspicious.

"You keep that girl," he said. "Anyone who goes out of her way to feed you on her break is a keeper."

"Yes, sir," I said.

We got busy. The kind of steady lunch that makes time pretend it's behaving. I bounced between tables, refills, "how's everything tasting," and the quiet calculus of who looked like they needed the check versus who wanted another beer and a reason to loiter. Twice, I almost repeated one of Bo's sarcastic comments out loud, catching myself just before I told a banker in a lavender dress shirt that "Your aura says you would like onion rings." Close call.

Between slinging plates, I froze for a second with a tray balanced on my palm. A draft slid through the doorway. It was sharp, sudden, and cold enough to prick my skin. Outside, the sun stayed where it was, but the light felt thinner. I looked up at the air conditioner. It wasn't running.

"Not normal," Bo said. No humor in it. "The wind is wrong."

"Wrong how?" I asked, smiling for table five as I set down their fish tacos.

"It smells like snow."

"It's September," I said automatically, which is not a rebuttal when the person telling you is an eight-hundred-year-old dragon.

I carried empty glasses back to the bar. The window over the river had frosted at the margins, just a whisker of lace that disappeared when I blinked, then crept back. On the far bank, the maples hadn't turned yet like the trees further north, but I watched a few leaves flip their pale undersides to the wind like cards revealing themselves in a Wild West saloon poker game. The tide eddied strangely, a few curls of current that didn't match the rest. Goosebumps climbed my forearms. I knew there wasn't a sea dragon out there anymore, but something just didn't feel right about it.

"Hey, Parker," I said, keeping it light as I leaned in to his office. "You got the heat set to 'as cold as a haunted house' today? It's as chilly out here."

He looked up from the office doorway. "Thermostat's off. You sure you're okay to work a double? Maybe you're coming down sick. I don't want you to miss any more work. I'm short-handed as it is."

"Fine," I said. "Just drafty, I guess."

"Storm coming," he said, like it was a fact he trusted because his arm with the prosthesis had a way of telling. He's good at reading the weather. He took a tour in a place where the weather was more than just a matter of needing an umbrella or not. Some of the desert sandstorms he had told me about were enough to bury a house. Not that Parker ever told many stories of his time in Iraq. "Finish your section and take ten. You look like you're about to pass out."

I wasn't. But my head was busy. The Hidden Path trial hadn't left a mark on my skin, but the part of me that listened to the world, the quiet listening that isn't ears, was still open and raw. The cold wasn't just cold. It was the kind that travels with purpose. As if someone opened a massive freezer door somewhere that should have stayed closed.

Blue Hair flagged me as I passed. "We need your professional opinion," she whispered. "Is it totally insane to do an episode at Fort Gorges at night?"

"Yes," I said immediately.

Lanky nodded solemnly. "So, we should do it at dusk."

"Eat your fries," I said, and moved on before I told them all to stay home forever. Not my job. Still my worry.

Outside, a gust slammed a stack of paper menus off the host stand. I crouched to gather them and realized my breath fogged the air in a thin plume. In September. Sunshine ticked off the water like nothing was wrong.

Bo appeared out of nowhere and leaned against my knee. "Mountain air," he said. "Smells wrong. It doesn't belong here."

"You think it's Pamola?" I muttered. "Reaching this far?"

"Not him," Bo said. "Something bigger. More. Something opening." He hesitated. "The little ones will know."

The Mikumwess. The thought of the Penobscot little people of the forest settled in my chest like a coin dropping into a jukebox, and my favorite song coming on. Of course. The "small ones" had built a trial from one of my childhood stories. They could read a forest's mood like Parker read a weather map.

I finished the lunch rush on muscle memory, hand to plate, plate to table, thank you, yes, I'll grab more napkins, be right back with that check, ma'am. The Haunt Hunters left me a coaster with their logo hand-stamped on it and a note: #BocephusForPresident . It wasn't even a custom coaster. They had stamped it on one of ours using an ink stamp they must have ordered online. I stuffed it into my apron and told myself not to look up their channel tonight. I would, though. I always do. Can't be too careful. I'll also need to check Etsy for #BocephusForPresident merchandise for sale.

Parker slid me a bowl when the tickets finally slowed down. Haddock chowder, extra pepper, a bag of oyster crackers, and two hunks of warm bread. He grabbed Valerie's sandwich and sat it next to the bowl.

"Staff meal," he said. "Sit." I did.

Bo stared. I broke a piece of bread and put it under the bar for him.

"Don't let customers see you feeding the dog in the restaurant," Parker said.

"He's a service animal," I said.

"For what?"

"Emotional stability," I said. Parker and Bo both snorted.

We ate in the slow time between lunch and the early dinner people who had a seven o'clock bedtime. The cold eased for a bit, but then tightened again like a midnight muscle spasm. That was when I saw the shadow pass over the window. Bird, cloud, memory, I don't know. It definitely wasn't a plane; we aren't in a flight path. When I looked up, there was nothing to be seen. The frost lace had melted, leaving drips that traced down the pane like someone had just stepped out of a hot shower and fogged the mirror.

Parker leaned on the bar. "You ever notice," he said, conversational, "how trouble has a way of showing up on a schedule you don't approve of?"

"Constantly," I said.

He nodded at the window. "Whatever's making you look out the window like that? Go handle it. I can manage with one less server tonight."

"I can finish my shift," I said, automatically defending myself.

"I know you can," he said. "That's not what I said. This isn't a choice."

Stand-in dad, boss, and platoon leader all rolled into one.

I cleaned my bowl, wiped the bar, and filled ketchup bottles because that kind of chore makes you feel useful even when you don't have anything else to do. Then I untied my apron and hung it on the peg behind the office door. That's the way Parker likes it. Neat and tidy, everything has a place.

On my way out, Blue Hair intercepted me by the hostess stand. "We'll DM you the Fort Gorges video," she whispered. "If you think it's too spicy, we can hold it."

"Hold it," I said, maybe too quickly. "And don't go out there until you've got someone with a clue out there with you." She misread the someone and grinned.

"That you?"

"No," I said. "Definitely not me," as I walked out the door, not waiting for a response. No games, I don't want Blue-Hair to mistake concern for flirting.

The sunlight outside felt thin and oddly weak, like one of those bright winter days when the sun sits high in the sky but doesn't seem to give off any heat. Bo kept pace at my heel, his tail flicking back and forth like a conductor keeping time for an unseen orchestra. The river made its usual sounds of water slapping against stone on the sides as it swirled and whorled its way to the sea.

I stopped at the rocks on the edge of the parking lot and let the view take over for a second. The broken smokestack was gone now, hauled away to salvage, but my eyes still drew to the space it left behind. We'd fought a sea dragon with an audience who didn't remember. We'd bargained with a storm god and walked a trial through a story I read in middle school. And here I was, letting people in polo shirts decide my tip based on whether their fries arrived hot.

I can't complain. It's a good life.

"Little ones," Bo said. No room left for joking. "Tonight."

"Tonight," I said.

"Then the mountain," he added.

"Then the mountain," I agreed, not anxious to go back. I shoved my hands into my jacket pockets and felt the coaster the Haunt Hunters had left me. #BocephusForPresident. I laughed out loud, and a stranger walking by looked at me like I was the oddest thing he'd seen all day. He wasn't wrong.

Behind me, the tavern door opened and closed, and the ordinary sounds of people drifted out. Inside, someone cheered. Probably a touchdown on the TV I always forget we have. Everyday life, doing what it does: keeping its rhythms, insisting on moving forward.

I started walking. The apartment wasn't far. Grandma's brownies waited in a Tupperware on the counter, because of course she'd sent me home with some. Valerie would come by at eight when she gets out of work. I'd call Red and John Patrick before that and let them know what Bo and I were planning to do next.

The wind shifted once more, quick and knife-cold, and then it was gone. A sudden icy straight-line blast that chilled me to the core. This time, it has hit me so hard it almost knocked me sideways. Not a threat. A reminder, sent directly to us.

Bo bumped my leg, setting me straight once again. "Bring snacks," he said.

"I always do," I said, feeling the power that existed between the two of us coursing through my veins, warming my chilled flesh. For the first time since we left the mountain, I felt ready.

"Those who dwell among the beauties and mysteries of the earth are never alone or weary of life."

Rachel Carson

CHAPTER EIGHTEEN

THE FEATHER OF ACCORD

By the time I reached Grandma's street, the sky had settled into an afternoon washed-out blue that made the maples look brighter than they had any right to. My legs still remembered the mountain, even if the rest of the world had decided to pretend storms were a rumor. Bo trotted ahead, ears flapping, and kept glancing back like he was making sure I wasn't about to fall through an invisible hole in the sidewalk.

"You look like wet laundry," he said into my head, voice dry as a dish towel.

"Thanks," I muttered. "Very supportive."

We cut across the lawn and up the little brick path that my grandfather laid a hundred years ago. Not literally, of course, even though he was apparently hundreds of years old and I never knew until The Protectors discovered his story. Before I could raise my hand to knock, the screen door sighed open and Grandma stood there in her flour-dusted apron, her gray hair gathered in an unbothered knot. She stepped aside and gave me a quick kiss on the cheek as we entered. It wasn't just the tightness around my eyes; she could see everything in the way I carried myself. The way I held my shoulders was like I was still waiting for thunder.

"There you are," she said, as if I'd simply wandered off in the neighborhood for the afternoon. "Wash your hands. The chowder's ready."

Chowder twice in one day. One haddock, one clam. Welcome to fall in Maine. Inside, the kitchen smelled of cream, clams, and cracked pepper. Bo did his usual polite trot to the table, sat as if the chair was his by birthright, and sniffed appreciatively.

"Good afternoon, Bocephus," Grandma said, bending to scratch behind his ear. She always used his full name, the way you speak to princes and dogs. "You may have a small bowl if you can refrain from slurping."

"I promise nothing," he said to only me, eyes gleaming.

I scrubbed my hands at the sink until they were pink, and when I turned, she'd already ladled the chowder into three bowls, set out thick slices of buttered bread, and put a plate of homemade zucchini pickles in the center like it was a holiday. She sat, waited for me to sit, and only then picked up her spoon.

We ate in that old rhythm that makes conversation unnecessary. Spoons clinking and the soft sigh of a house that has settled into its bones. After a while, she said, lightly, "You've got that look your grandfather used to wear when he came home from the mountain."

I wanted to jump directly to the million questions that came to mind about Grandpa and Mount Katahdin. This was something new to me.

"What look is that?" I asked instead.

"The one that says the sky shouted at you and you shouted back, and neither of you won." She tore a piece of bread and handed it to Bo, who took it with uncharacteristic gentleness. "You don't have to tell me, Wilder. But you can."

I stared into the chowder. Fat little rafts of butter gleamed like tiny suns floating in the white chowder.

"He's...not a story," I said finally. "Pamola. He's not a myth or weather or a carved sign on a trailhead. He's a presence that gets under your skin. I thought ..." I stopped, because it sounded foolish to say it out loud. "I thought being a Protector would make me bigger than fear."

"Mm." She sipped, thoughtful. "Your grandfather thought the same. He learned fear and respect are cousins, not enemies."

Bo thumped his tail once. "She's not wrong."

I blew out a breath. "There are hikers up there. Kids. Families. He's not trying to kill anyone, not exactly, but fear makes accidents, and accidents pile up. I need him to stop. I need him to listen."

Grandma set her spoon down. The light through the window made a thin halo of steam around her head. "Finish your chowder," she said, and there was a shift in her voice I recognized from childhood. Grandma's tone meant we were about to cross a threshold.

"Then I'll show you something of your grandfather's."

We ate quietly the rest of the meal. The music playing quietly from the radio on the counter was the only noise in the room. After Bo licked his bowl clean enough to pass a health inspection, Grandma rose and wiped her hands on a dish towel. She didn't go to the cupboard with the teacups like she usually would after dinner. She went to the bedroom at the back of the house, the one that still smelled faintly of cedar and old cologne, and returned carrying the small carved chest I'd only ever seen when she dusted.

"I'm sure you realize by now that I knew all about your Grandpa George's life before me. Quite a few lives, you could say. Even when he first told me, I loved him enough to know it was all true, despite the lack of evidence. I knew that he had lived and loved many women before me, and that we weren't his first family. His life was not an easy one, even after he walked away from his role. He always watched and waited, always stayed connected in his own way. Last summer, when you told me about the elderly gentlemen you had been spending time with playing cards and such, it didn't take me long to put two and two together. I had heard stories for years about their adventures and exploits over the centuries, as Protectors, and the important role they played in keeping our world safe. I'd heard the names of those men so many times in George's stories," she let out a little laugh. "When you sat at this very table and told me their names, all three of them together, I could almost feel your grandfather's presence grow in the room. Your role was predetermined, Wilder. No matter how much anyone tried to keep you from it, fate always has a way of coming out on top."

She set the chest on the table with both palms. It was wider than her woven placemat, as wide as her shoulders. Swiping her hand across the top as if greeting an old friend, she worked the brass clasp with a thumb that knew exactly where to press. Inside were familiar things—a packet of letters tied with blue ribbon, a compass with a cracked face, the pocketknife with the bone handle I'd once been allowed to hold but not open. Beneath those, wrapped in unbleached muslin, was something long and slender.

Grandma unwound the cloth. The kitchen dimmed around the edges as my focus intensified.

It was a feather, as large as the chest it had just come out of. Not merely large, but longer than my forearm, the vane broad and flawless, the quill opalescent. Its color shifted as it moved:

storm-gray until the light skated across it, making it flash with oil-slick blues and a thin, dangerous white at the fringe. I could smell rain. Not water, not wet earth—*rain*, the first clean sheet of it before it hits anything.

The air around it held a hush I felt in my teeth, the way a room quiets just before a symphony begins. The hair on my arms lifted in the moment of anticipation, as when the conductor taps his baton just before the orchestra plays.

Bo stood up so fast his chair squeaked. "That is not a bird I have eaten," he said reverently. And out loud.

Grandma's mouth quirked. "No, I imagine not."

It was the first time she had ever heard Bo speak out loud, but she showed no sign of being surprised. Most people would have run from the room screaming about the possessed dog sitting at their kitchen table, and nobody would ever believe their story.

"What is it?" I asked, though I somehow already knew.

She held the feather up by the tip of the quill and twirled it in her fingers. Her voice softened the way it does when you say a name you haven't said in years. "Your grandfather called it the Feather of Accord."

I reached without thinking, then stopped, hands hovering.

"You won't break it," she said. "Objects like this don't belong to us, strictly speaking. They only let themselves be kept."

I lifted the feather. It was as light as a feather should be, yet heavier than my hand could explain. The edge caught the light and threw it back as if the feather had its own small sun trapped inside. It glowed.

"When?" I asked. "What ... how ..." The questions had too many roots. When did Grandpa George tell her? When did they decide it should be kept?

"Before you were born, but long after he should have been done with the mountain," she said. "He went up because a boy wandered off the trail, and the weather had turned. He came back with frost in his beard in July and that feather tucked into his coat sleeve." She took a breath, and for a moment I saw the woman she had been. Her face unlined, hands quick, waiting with concern at a window for a figure to emerge from tree shadow.

"He would not say he won anything. He said he asked. Nicely."

"Pamola gave it to him?"

"Pamola allowed it to be given," she said carefully. "Your grandfather said it like that. Allowed. He told me the Mikumwess stood at the edge of the clearing, not smiling for once, and that the wind pushed his words back into his mouth until he found a different tone. He said the feather was not payment. It was proof. Proof of understanding each other."

I turned it slowly. As I did, the kitchen's noises shifted. The clock's tick tock fell slightly out of step, the refrigerator hum dipped, the space between breaths lengthened like a held note. When I stilled my hand, everything snapped back, ordinary as salt.

"What does it do?" I whispered.

"Nothing," she said, and something in me relaxed at the honesty of it. "And everything. When your grandfather held it, storms calmed faster. Old voices quieted. The hungry things in the trees paused and looked at him. He said it didn't command. It convinced. It told the old beings he carried respect first."

Bo edged closer, pupils wide. "May I?"

I lowered the tip until it hovered over his forehead. He didn't touch it. He didn't have to. The fur along his spine rose in a tidy ridge and then flattened again, and for a heartbeat, his brown eyes were wholly gold.

"It smells like sky," he said softly. "And like ancient rules."

Grandma smiled at Bo, "I always knew there was more to you than meets the eye, Bocephus." His expression turned more wistful as she continued, "George said there would be a day when someone ... you, Wilder; he said your name, would need to show they did not come with blade or flame first. He said... 'When the mountain grows restless again, give this to the one with a steadier heart than mine.'"

I looked down at the quill and saw my reflection laddered in the sheen—thin, blurred, human. The room felt tiny and enormous at once, the way it does when you stand in a doorway and can't decide whether you are leaving or coming home.

"What do I do with it?" I asked. "How do I use it without ... using it?"

"You carry it," she said simply. "You show it. You speak as your grandfather learned to speak. Without hurry, without demand. He told me there are words, old ones, but he also said they are not a spell to be pronounced correctly so much as a promise to be kept. The Mikumwess would know them if you asked. But Wilder?" She waited until I met her eyes. "If you mean what you say, the feather will make it easier to hear. That's all it does. It makes listening possible."

Bo huffed, which might have been agreement. Or indigestion.

Grandma wrapped the muslin the rest of the way and set the Feather of Accord back into my hands, this time for good. It didn't feel like receiving a weapon. It felt like accepting a chore you should have been doing all along.

We sat there for a while, not talking much. She poured tea. She cut more brownies. They were still warm, the top crackled and shiny. She pushed two onto my plate without asking and put two more on a plate in front of Bo. The house returned to its usual tempo: clock, fridge, the tiny tick of cooling pans. Outside, a jay made a noise like a hinge that needed oiling. Grandma got up for a moment and opened the screen door, tossing out a handful of peanuts.

"Keeps them busy," she laughed. "They are noisy birds."

When I stood to leave, she fussed with my collar and made a show of checking my pockets like I was eight. Then she pulled me into a hug that smelled like Oil of Olay soap and said into my shoulder, very quietly, "You have your grandfather's stubbornness, but your own way with people. That will matter more than the first. Remember the gifts he gave to you. They are more than what they seem."

I eased back, trying not to look like someone on the verge of crying over baked goods. "Did he ever ..." I started, then stopped. Too many questions. Always too many.

She patted my cheek. "Later. There's always time for stories. Today you have a little hike to plan, and a storm to talk to."

At the door, Bo paused and looked up at her as much as his stubby neck would allow. She bent, as if confiding something scandalous to a conspirator. "And you, sir, mind your temper. No dragoning around if you can help it." She did know.

"I am the Chewbacca to his Han Solo," he said gravely, which made her laugh.

"I don't know what that means, but I know you'll watch out for each other."

We stepped onto the porch. The afternoon had that thin shine Maine sometimes gets, where everything is in focus at once. I tucked the wrapped feather into my pack and felt the strap settle differently across my shoulder, as if I'd balanced a scale. It weighed nothing and a thousand pounds at the same time, but there were no adverse physical effects to carrying it. Only ... assurance.

"Wilder?" Grandma called. I turned. She stood in the frame of the screen door, a silhouette against the warm square of the kitchen. "Whatever voice you use up there, make sure it's yours."

"I will."

The door whispered shut. The feather lay quiet against my spine, and for the first time since Pamola's shadow had crossed the summit, I could imagine speaking without shouting.

Bo bumped my calf and took two steps towards the forest path. "What about the little ones?"

"We are ready," I said as I walked toward the street. "I think they'll be there if we need them."

Chapter Nineteen

Valerie's Surprise

"I have all my things packed!" Valerie was excited, pointing to the rolling suitcase on the floor of her apartment.

"Wow, I didn't realize you were so serious," I said without a trace of concern in my voice. I wanted her to think this would be a fun fall hiking adventure. When I texted Valerie on the walk back from Grandma's house to let her know we were on the way home but would be heading back to Katahdin tomorrow, I was surprised when she said she would love to come along with us.

"It'll be such a fun adventure. You always have great stories to tell about your hikes and getting back to nature, so I thought it would be wonderful to share the experience. You sure you don't mind?"

"Of course not," I replied. How exactly was this supposed to work, I wondered. I'm headed to the mountain with Bo to confront a legendary Native American thunder god, and my girlfriend wants to tag along for the 'fun.' There's no backing out now, and I don't want to make Valerie mad. I want her to stay in my life. I'll figure out something as we go along, but I don't want her to be in any danger.

Valerie looked at me, hand on her hip, with her head cocked sideways. That special way she looks at me that always means a surprise is coming, and I didn't see it arrive.

"I'm just kidding, silly. You and Bo have a great time. I'm taking the train to Boston to visit my parents for the weekend. I don't want to interrupt your boys trip." She let out a laugh. "You always come back smelly and dirty. That doesn't sound like much fun to me!"

Holy mackerel. She got me on that one.

I let out a huge laugh, "Are you sure? You're always welcome. There's plenty of room on the three-inch mattress at the old motel in Millinocket. They have running water and flush toilets up there, contrary to popular belief."

"The answer is still no," she said. "I can tell you enjoy the time by yourself."

Enjoy may be a little strong. I'm getting ready to fly to the top of a mountain, hopefully not get blasted by lightning and hurricane-force winds, and then have a friendly tete-a-tete with an ancient god. I should probably pack some toilet paper and a few extra pairs of underwear.

Bo heard the thought in my head and let out a laugh. It only sounded like a few low woofs to Valerie, but she gave him a sideways glance anyway.

"What's up with Bo? Is he okay?"

"I don't know, Bo, ARE you okay?" I asked with extra emphasis. Valerie chuckled at the exchange.

"You two really are something special. Anyway, dinner is ready. I just got out of work, so I made a couple of chicken parm sandwiches with extra mozzarella. Easy-peasy. They're in the kitchen. I got that Italian red wine you like, too."

We sat and talked, laughing about our day and enjoying each other's company and a few glasses of wine. I had needed an ordinary day. Even though my visit with Grandmas was far from ordinary, at least my day had started routinely and was ending in the most comfortably relaxing way possible.

After dinner, we chilled on the couch and watched a movie. Neither of us paid much attention to the plot as we talked, and Bo snoozed quietly in the dog bed Valerie had in the corner for him. The end of the evening came all too soon.

"Be safe on your hike," Valerie said as she kissed us both goodnight at the door. "Make sure you dress warmly. You think we've had a weird cold snap here ... I checked the forecast for the top of Mount Katahdin, and temps are supposed to be in the forties up at the top. Not much warmer at the base."

"I promise to pack warm clothes," I reassured her. I knew the weather could be a lot worse than that if Pamola didn't like our visit.

CHAPTER TWENTY

UNEXPECTED GUESTS

I did dress warmly, because we decided to travel the quickest way possible. That means flying, and it's not warm a thousand feet up this time of year. I wore my long black wool coat, gloves, a scarf, goggles, and a winter hat. I was ready for a blizzard but hoping there wouldn't actually be one. A dragon radiated enough body heat that I barely felt a chill for the flight to Millinocket, the closest town to Baxter State Park and the mountain. I had another reservation at the Pamola Peak Inn. Not fancy, but easy to hide a dragon in.

"Bo, do you see what I see?" I asked him as we flew over the motel, getting ready to land out back where nobody would see us.

"A herd of cats?" he asked. "I hope so."

"We can get a late breakfast at the diner, relax. I mean that truck in the parking lot out front. It looks like Red's pickup."

"I can feel them here," Bo replied. "Can't you? They are both nearby."

He was right. All I had to do was reach out with a little bit of magic and I could feel the presence of the two other Protectors. Red and John Patrick were here in Millinocket, parked in front of the motel.

They honked the horn and greeted us as we walked around the corner of the building.

John Patrick was the first to wave a meaty hand out the truck passenger window, "Surprise, boyo and wee doggie!" He let out a massive laugh. "D'ye think you can take on a task like this without any backup from lads like us?"

Red stepped out of the truck and closed the door, making that clunk-clang sound that old trucks always make when the door and the frame don't quite meet perfectly.

"We're a team, Wilder. This is something new to all of us, and we're in this together."

"After I check into my room, we need to grab a quick breakfast. I have a story to catch you up on, and I think you're going to be surprised." They didn't know about Grandpa George and his confrontation and arrangement with Pamola. Until recently, they didn't even know Grandpa George had lived in the same town. Red and John Patrick thought he had left a few hundred years ago when he resigned as a Protector. Wizards tend to have long lives, unless something horrible happens.

After a few stacks of pancakes at our favorite North Woods diner, we went out for a bit of shopping. It turned out that Red and John Partick hadn't considered the weather when they made the rash decision to drive up to the park. The top of Mount Katahdin can be deadly in September. The weather could be sunny and sixty-five at the peak, or it might be thirty degrees Fahrenheit with sideways sleet and hurricane-force winds. A person could die quickly if they aren't prepared. Even a wizard can die from exposure.

Rhonda, our breakfast waitress, happily suggested the Katahdin General Store when we asked about buying some warmer clothes.

"The weather has turned cold, but my friends have decided to stay a few extra days," I said to her, nodding toward Red and John Patrick.

"They've got a great selection of everything you need. Coats, boots, gloves, whatever. There are some brochures in the rack by the door on your way out with a ten percent-off coupon, too. Say hi to my dad, he runs the place. His name's Vern. Tell him I sent you, and he'll double the discount."

Millinocket, Maine: Population 4,011. Small-town service can't be beat.

CHAPTER TWENTY-ONE

WHISPERS OF THE FOREST

We decided to all take Red's truck up to the trailhead and hike from there. Bo and I rode in the bed of the truck, like kids used to do back a generation ago. Nobody up here bats an eye when they see something like that. At home, the cops would be all over you like flies on a manure pile. I'm not saying it's safe, I'm just saying it happens. It was also a poor choice considering how bumpy the roads are. The few miles from the motel to the trailhead weren't exactly the most comfortable, with only the metal truck bed under me. I was already starting what promised to be an arduous day with sore muscles.

The path wound up the mountain, slowly but surely. The trail widened and narrowed between spruces, birch, and firs. The trees sometimes leaned in as if they were eavesdropping on our conversations. Colored leaves dropped, reminding us that fall had arrived in this part of the forest, and often surprised us with the motion from overhead. We were all hypersensitive to any activity around us. Being dressed for winter had proved to be a good idea since the air had a chill colder than it had any right to be in September. Any sudden breaths were cold and sharp, a reminder to stay in control of every physical aspect of our climb. It wouldn't do us any good to reach the summit and confront Pamola gasping and wheezing like a hockey player who should have retired a decade ago.

Red and John Patrick had no problem maintaining pace with us on the trail. They were deceptively fit. Since the day I had met them, they had been pillars of strength and in-spiration to me. Today was no different. They conversed in low voices between themselves, murmuring about the trail, the storm they could feel building above us, and the legends we were facing that had suddenly stopped being legends and become all too real.

Bo trotted next to me, mostly comment-free. It was odd for him not to be his usual sarcastic and smug self. His eyes flicked back and forth across the trail ahead as his ears twitched side-to-side, not missing a single sound. In my own chest, I could feel the low growl that sat in his, unreleased but ready for action.

Without warning or fanfare, the trail ahead of us filled with the small guardians of the forest. The Mikumwess had arrived. They stepped from behind tree trunks and rose up from behind moss-covered stones on either side of the trail. Their presence left me both comforted and wary at the same time.

The elder with whom I had spoken many times before stepped forward. His white beard caught the breeze as he approached. "The trees whisper of a great sorrow," he said, his voice quiet but carrying like wind through branches.

Another added, "The winds carry tales of giants awakening from their slumber."

Through his long life, Red had seen more impossible things than most men would believe, and even he let out a low whistle. "Ice giants," he whispered. "The Kiwakwa have returned."

John Patrick's Scottish brogue got even thicker when he muttered, "Saints preserve us. It's good we are all here together."

The Mikumwess stepped into a loose single-file line next to us on the trail and began to sing as we all walked. There was no tune you could hum along with, no verses or chorus. Just steady lines that lingered in the air as they were sung.

The trees remember, the trees remember, Roots in sorrow, roots in stone. Cold wind rising, cold wind rising, Giants stirring, not alone.

Branches creaked overhead as the cold wind passed through them. The air grew colder as our elevation increased. The ground still held a bit of the summer's warmth, but the air had moved on to the next season. There would surely be a frost tonight.

John Patrick cleared his throat, "They're tellin' us what's comin', laddie."

The elder Mikumwess turned his head toward us and nodded. "Long ago, the Kiwakwa were bound by the spirits of the forest. But the chains of magic weaken, and they stir once more."

Another Mikumwess lifted his face to the sky and began a new chant.

Step with the forest, breathe with the pine, Walk with the river, the mountain is mine. Fire and shadow, storm and sky, Balance unbroken, or all will die.

Bo bumped his head again on my leg, letting a bit of the growl out, "I know these names. The ice giants were even known to dragons, halfway across the world. Cold that burned hotter than fire. They were beings even dragons feared."

That sent a chill through me deeper than the wind.

The Mikumwess elder reached up and placed a hand on my shoulder, heavy as a rock despite his small stature. "Wilder Blackwood, you must go to Pamola. He will hear you now, because we ask it. The giants are not his concern. They are ours."

Red stepped forward, jaw set as solid and confident as a President carved on Mount Rushmore. "Then it falls to me and John Patrick. We've fought worse. Maybe not bigger, but worse."

John Patrick replied in his special way, leaving you wondering if he was offended or humored. "Speak for yourself, old man."

I wanted to face these problems together, but there were two obstacles in our way, and no single solution existed. We needed to split up to be effective as a team.

The Mikumwess sang once more, their voices fitting together like the branches overhead.

Chains are breaking, ice is waking, Hear the thunder, hear the flame. Kiwakwa rising, Kiwakwa calling, Guard the forest, speak their name.

Thunder rolled high above us, even though the sky was the clear cerulean blue of a perfect September day in Maine. I would have sworn the ground trembled under my feet, as if the mountain itself was reacting to the words of their song.

Bo looked up at me, his eyes flashing golden and fiery. I saw a ripple pass along his spine, his body begging to transform now. "We face the storm god. They face the giants."

He was right, and we all had come to the same conclusion.

I looked at Red and John Patrick with the Mikumwess circling them like guardians and felt the weight of the choice settle. They would be in safe hands and fully capable of defending themselves regardless.

"Then let's do it," I said.

The mountain had presented its tasks for us, and we were ready to accept the challenges.

The eldest Mikumwess stopped and turned to me.

"You carry an item with you that is rare and beautiful. It will help you achieve peace and harmony."

The feather.

He continued, "It does not force peace. It only reveals the truth of someone's heart when offered. Give it to Pamola when the storm rages most. It will not shield you from judgment. But it will show him whether you come in greed or in accord."

"When the dragon's breath meets the mountain's snow, storms are born."

Korean proverb

CHAPTER TWENTY-TWO

MEETING THE PAST

We split at the next fork in the trail. The Mikumwess accompanied Red and John Patrick as they headed to find the Kiwakwa. Bo and I continued the climb up the mountain to speak to Pamola. The world is a very different place than it used to be, and his guardianship of the mountain needs to be adjusted accordingly. I hope he will be able to see it my way. There was once a time when the mountain could be forbidden territory, but now there needs to be an understanding of access for all. Pamola can't just make people vanish because they hiked up the mountain or accidentally littered or thought about bottling some mountain spring water. Even if they had hostile intentions, there are other ways to prevent people and corporations from exploiting the area's natural resources.

"Why do we walk?" Bo asked a very decent question.

"Well ... so Red and John Patrick can walk with us to see Pamola."

"They are with the little ones."

"Valid point," I admitted. "The trees have thinned out a bit. Do you think that little clearing over there is big enough for you to go dragon on us? We'll get there a lot faster."

Bo didn't waste any time hopping roots and fallen sticks, trotting over to the boulder-littered clearing. There couldn't have been more than fifteen feet of clearance on either side, but the scrawny trees around us weren't much more than ten feet high. The clearing was mostly surrounded by scrub brush since not much grew at this altitude.

Bo hopped up onto a granite boulder the size of a small car. In a flash, Bo went from little Frenchie to massive ancient dragon, his red scales glinting in the sunshine. The rush of displaced air blew my hair back and made me stagger a step, but it could have been the pure joy I felt whenever I saw him transform. Sometimes he took his sweet time, relishing in the moment. Other times, it was as sudden and powerful as an explosion. Dog to dragon in mere seconds. The boulder sank another foot, the weight of an Earth Dragon sinking it into the ground.

Bo stretched his wings, tips touching the trees around us. "Let's go."

I climbed from the dragon's knee to his back, settling into my rider position. As I clenched the spikes protruding from his neck, I squeezed my knees in for a better grip and took a deep breath. After flipping up the collar of my long coat and pulling my goggles down over my eyes, I was ready.

"Let's ride the sky."

Ten seconds later, the entire region was within our range of view. From Knife's Edge near the peak of Katahdin to the far-off squat buildings and shuttered factories in Millinocket.

We communicated with thoughts, since the icy wind stole the breath from my lungs when I tried to speak out loud.

"Bo, we saw the ice giants a while ago when we were in the Klondike. They even chased us through the forest. Why do you think they stopped and let us go?"

"Pamola. Always Pamola."

"The storm that grounded us that day was sent by Pamola. The Kiwakwa chased us as a ... warning?"

"Nothing happens on this mountain without Pamola allowing it. Or creating it"

Storm clouds gathered at the base of the mountain, not far from where we had been hiking. The dark, angry clouds were even more noticeable to us as we flew above them, obscuring the forest below. The sun had been shining when we parted ways with the rest of the gang, but now the storm had popped up, small and centralized, a sure sign that it wasn't natural. It was Pamola's creation. The entire storm system was only a mile in diameter. That's not natural.

"Bo, I know we need to bring Pamola up to date on the last century of humanity, but take a look at that storm down there. I think we're headed in the wrong direction. He's there, with Red and John Patrick."

"Leading us away, maybe."

"But we need to make sure they are okay. They can't face the Kiwakwa and Pamola on their own, even with the help of the Mikumwess."

"The little ones will not take a side."

"I think you're right, but they will steer us in the right direction."

We descended quickly, gaining speed as we approached the stormy area. Bo leveled out above the treetops, gliding under the layer of clouds. It was a whitewash of snow. Here, in the shadow of Mount Katahdin in September, was a full-on blizzard like you'd see in the middle of January.

I pulled my grandfather's pocketwatch from the inside pocket of my coat, letting it dangle from the gold chain. He had enchanted it a few hundred years ago as a way of tracking the Protectors. They weren't happy when they learned about it, but at the time we had bigger fish to fry. We discovered it when we were searching for the sea dragon threatening our city. The watch spun in the fierce cold wind before settling in with a very discernible lean.

"That way," I signaled to Bo. "Head to the right. East, I mean. The watch will lead us."

The storm was small in size, but it carried the kind of violence that made it feel alive. The snow and winds were howling, biting, and furious. Icy needles of snow rattled off my goggles like dirt road gravel and sliced across my exposed cheeks with razor-sharp sting. Mental note: gloves. Next time, wear gloves. My fingers felt like stiff twigs clutching at Bo's scales, but at least his body burned with heat, a living furnace against the storm's teeth. Holding onto him was like gripping a heated steering wheel that was warm and alive under my palms.

At Bo's urging, I tuned into his dragon sight, the world suddenly sharpening and glowing in impossible hues. Two sets of eyes scanned the blizzard until we spotted them. His voice rumbled in my head, steady despite the chaos.

"Ahead. I'm going in."

Through the swirl of snow, I saw them too. They were in a clearing huddled against the base of a cliff, its fifty-foot face breaking the storm's worst fury. The wind clawed at us as we twisted through the air, Bo's wings fighting every gust and surge. My stomach lurched with each jagged drop.

"Rough landing ahead," he warned.

He wasn't exaggerating. We dropped like a stone, slamming into the frozen ground just yards from Red and John Patrick. Both men stood braced, blades raised and gleaming under the storm's gray light, their faces hard with focus. Beside them, the Mikumwess had gathered, bare-chested despite the weather. The storm raged, but snow swirled harmlessly around their bodies, as though the blizzard could not touch them. They were part of the forest.

And across the clearing, the Kiwakwa waited. Oh good. I was worried this hike was getting boring.

There was at least a dozen of them watching our group. Each one a mountain of muscle and ice. Their eyes were cold and luminous, burning with hunger. I had heard the legends, and these living legends are deadly. There would be no happy ending if they caught any of us. When we had first been chased by them only weeks ago, they blended with the trees. Now they were stripped of camouflage and looked as though winter itself had grown legs and decided to walk.

"Like the apple trees in Wizard of Oz, but deadlier," Bo offered.

"I'll say it again, Bo. Too much TV."

As a warning, Bo roared. It shook the clearing, louder than the storm. He unleashed a line of flame that split the snow in two, scorching a barrier across the earth like a fiery "Do Not Cross" sign. Fire hissed and spat against ice, the smoke writhing upward only to be torn apart by the wind. His meaning was simple: cross this line, and you'll burn.

The Kiwakwa didn't flinch. They still stepped forward, slow and deliberate, the crunch of their massive feet echoing off the cliff behind us. Bo's trench of flame burned across the clearing between us, the undergrowth providing a rich source of fuel for the fire. If this had been in drier weather, the entire clearing would be ablaze by now.

Bo roared threateningly again, his entire body shaking with the energy and power he was preparing to unleash.

"Hold back, buddy. We need to tread lightly up here."

"More brains, less brawn," he responded.

I had expected to find Pamola at the heart of this storm, not the Kiwakwa. They must have been awakened by the same unknown changes that Pamola spoke to us about. Whatever brought the mountain spirit back into the modern world must have also awakened the ice giants. But fighting them could possibly anger Pamola, and we were here to make peace. I tapped my hand against the breast of my long coat to feel the comforting bulge of the package containing the Feather of Accord.

"We can't lose sight of the plan," I reminded Bo.

Bo unleashed another furious jet of fire across the burning clearing, increasing the flames where they had begun to diminish and igniting more areas that had gone out. The wall of flame stretched high above the ground, over a man's head, but not as tall as the walking trees that wanted to tear us apart.

The Mikumwess began their chant. Their voices were high and sharp, threading through the howl of the storm, weaving together like spaghetti strands of silver light. Power shimmered in the air around us, invisible walls taking shape as protective wards. The storm bent away, snowflakes veering off course as if striking glass. For the first time since we landed, I could breathe without ice clawing into my lungs.

But the giants kept coming.

Chapter Twenty-Three

Remember the Hidden Path

Maybe it was only my imagination, but the air around us seemed to drop another degree with every step they took closer. Their eyes locked on us, and I felt the weight of their hunger. They weren't just here to fight. They wanted to consume, to swallow fire and magic and life until nothing remained but more ice. Some say they are cursed humans twisted by greed or betrayal, others that they are ogres with an endless hunger for flesh. Either way, wherever they tread, the storm follows. And the storm always kills.

Bo growled low, his scales pulsing with heat under my grip. Red shifted his stance, jaw clenched, and John Patrick muttered "Alba gu bràth" before raising his sword higher. Even with the Mikumwess chanting behind us, the clearing felt smaller by the second. The Kiwakwa's howls split the clearing, and the Protectors braced for battle. Red's longsword gleamed in the reflected flames, noble and mythical. John Patrick's shorter arming sword fit him better—more brawler than knight, ready to mix swordplay with brute force.

That's when I noticed what they were protecting. Not treasure. People.

A cluster of figures huddled near the cliff wall, a dozen in all. Boys, no older than fifteen, their scout uniforms covered with ice. A couple of troop leaders stood with them, trying to shield the kids with nothing more than their bodies. Their faces were pale with cold and terror. Red and John Patrick weren't just holding the line for themselves, they were trying to keep these kids alive.

Red yelled to me above the howling wind, "We found them lost in the storm. We need to get them to safety."

My stomach dropped. The Kiwakwa weren't just a threat to us. They were about to rip through an entire troop of hikers who'd taken a wrong turn into the worst possible nightmare.

"Bo," I muttered.

"I see them," he rumbled. His scales flared with heat. "We'll have to move fast."

The scouts looked terrified, as they should have. Not only were they trapped in a mysterious snow squall unlike any that had ever happened before, but they were also being protected by two men older than their grandpas, both wielding swords. And then there's the giant red dragon, the walking ice giants that look like trees came to life, and a wizard wearing ski goggles. They were putting on a brave face, standing tall and ready to face the danger. Some of the boys had cut walking sticks on their hike, and now they held them like weapons. A few gripped pocketknives. In a display of grit, they stepped out from behind Red and John Patrick, forming a line across the far end of the clearing. Bravest kids I'd ever seen.

Then the Kiwakwa howled. It wasn't human; it was the shriek of glaciers grinding against stone. The sound buried itself in my ears and rattled my bones. I had heard it once before, and it nearly killed me then. Hearing it again was even worse.

One of them strode forward and stepped straight through Bo's fire line. The flames licked at its shins like sparks from a dying campfire, sputtering and guttering to ash. The giant's eyes burned colder than the ice storm around us, and it crushed the embers beneath its heel. For a heartbeat, I thought we were done. Great. This is how it ends. Not with a bang, but with a freezer-burn popsicle scream.

Then, with a massive ear-splitting crack of thunder, the storm changed.

The sky ripped open above us, clawed like paper beneath an eagle's talon. Lightning revealed wings unfurling, feathers black as midnight and tipped with frost. The wind punched harder, carrying a sound older than thunder and heavier than the granite bedrock of the mountain. Pamola, the storm's spir-it, had joined the party.

He had brought this storm, and he had allowed the Kiwak-wa to come back from legend.

He perched on the cliff like a god carved from storm and mountain, talons gouging stone, eyes flashing with lightning. Every giant froze where it stood. Even Bo went still beneath me, his body tense in anticipation. One apex ancient power facing another.

Pamola spread his wings, and the storm itself bowed.

His voice echoed across the clearing as he directed his words to me. His ancient eyes burned with a fire of untold ages, glowing wildly. The wind had dropped to a mere breeze, and the snow ceased completely.

"Why should I allow men on this mountain, when they leave ruin in their wake?"

The silence hung in the air for a moment. The question was rhetorical, and meant for me. But I had waited too long to answer. Pamola vanished, and the wind rose in force again. He was going to allow this attack to continue.

The Kiwakwa moved in silence this time, stepping across the flaming barricade. Bits and pieces of debris and detritus clinging to them briefly blazed up as they made their way to our side of the clearing. They were only twenty feet away, and their muted movement was more frightening than it should have been. Red and John Patrick stepped forward, increasing the distance between them and the boys in order to keep them as far as possible from the fighting that was about to begin.

The scouts began to scream, but not in fear. I turned and saw them, shouting and yelling, jumping up and down like warriors psyching themselves up for battle. This was like a scene from Braveheart, but there was no Mel Gibson to give them an inspiring speech.

One of the Mikumwess stopped chanting and turned to me. "Remember the hidden path."

Right. Magic wasn't about blasting fireballs until the bad guys tapped out. It was about balance. Survival. Protecting people. The Mikumwess had made that clear. True power meant working with what already existed, not twisting it into something unnatural.

I could feel the Kiwakwa pressing closer, and it was happening quickly. Their hunger felt like a claw at my chest, and every part of me screamed to fight back. But that wasn't the lesson. If I were to use magic now, it had to be to shield, not to destroy. To save the people behind me, not scorch the things in front of me.

The answer came to me in a flash. Reaching deep into myself to pull up all of the magic I could muster, I reached both hands toward the cliff above the advancing Kiwakwa. I had to get this right or the outcome would be messy. The stony outcropping fifty feet above them began to shake, trembling as it tried to hold its place. I pushed harder, willing the rocks to fall, but it couldn't just be downward. I needed the avalanche to fall away from the base of the cliff.

I reached deep past the fear and doubt into the reservoir of magic I'd been fighting against for the last few months. The mountain itself seemed to hum in my ears. I pulled it forward. Not lightning, not fire, but something raw and earthbound.

The cliff groaned above us. Pebbles tumbled, then the rocks tore free as I pushed harder, Bo's power surging into mine. The avalanche fell forward, well away from the boys and Protectors pressed against the cliff, tucking themselves back against the rock.

The avalanche crashed outward, hurling stone into the gap between us and the advancing Kiwakwa. The earth shook with each impact, until a jagged barricade of granite stretched from tree line to tree line like the wall of a fortress.

Twenty feet in front of the wide-eyed, cheering group, the mountain itself had sealed a line in the snow: us on one side, the giants on the other. A choking cloud of stone dust roared upward, swallowing the clearing, whipped into a swirling haze by the shrieking wind. Through the storm and the haze, the ice giants glared, their silhouettes frozen against the shifting wall. They were blocked, but not beaten.

The cheering scouts high-fived each other, wide-eyed but alive. I don't know how they weren't freaking out, but their tenacity was extraordinary.

Bo exhaled hard, smoke trailing from his nostrils. "Nicely done."

The air stilled, and the dust began to settle. And then Pamola was there again, wings half-folded, watching from what remained of the cliff's edge.

This time, there was something different in his gaze. It wasn't anger or disdain, but perhaps … respect.

"You found a way to shield even those who do not belong to you," he said, voice low and resonant. "You chose to preserve the creatures of this land instead of attempting to destroy them. Perhaps there is more to you, Wilder Blackwood, than ruin."

I exhaled deeply, my breath a plume of smoke in the frigid air as I prepared a response. I searched deep within myself for the answer. I needed to say the right thing, there would be no second chance. I remembered my grandmother's words.

Whatever voice you use up there, make sure it's yours."

I dismounted from Bo's back and stepped to a large flat rock that had fallen from the cliff. Reaching into my coat, I pulled out the wrapped package containing the Feather of Accord. Gently, reverently, I placed the feather on the rock in front of me in plain sight for Pamola, watching from fifty feet above.

"I cannot force you to trust me. I can only promise balance. This feather holds truth. Judge me by what you see in it."

Pamola studied the Feather as it glowed softly. He was silent for a long time. I hoped he could see my intention, and that not all men meant danger and destruction for the mountain.

"This is not the first time I have seen this gift. It was given to another, your blood. He offered truth, as you do now."

My chest tightened. Grandpa George.

Pamola extended one talon and tapped the air. The feather lifted from the rock as if pulled by an unseen current. It floated toward him, resting against his chest before vanishing into the darkness of his plumage.

"You have walked the Hidden Path. You have held fast to your bond. And now, you have offered truth instead of power. The mountain accepts you."

I let out a breath I didn't realize I'd been holding. Red and John Patrick lowered their swords in unison.

Pamola's gaze softened. "This mountain still holds meaning for your people. They no longer hear it as they once did, yet the bond between humans and this land endures. I will allow them to walk its paths and feel my spirit here."

Now we were getting somewhere.

"Does that mean you won't kill anyone else if you think they don't have the mountain's best interests at heart?"

He continued in his commanding but gentle voice, "Guard this mountain as I have, Wilder Blackwood, and the balance will remain. I will always be watching."

Knowing how hard the state already works to preserve the pristine nature of Baxter State Park and the area surrounding the mountain, I didn't have anything to worry about.

Pamola's next statement took me by surprise.

"I will return those whom I have taken. Humans need not be afraid of the mountain."

The missing hikers appeared out of nowhere next to the Protectors. All five of them, disheveled and stunned, but alive.

"You didn't kill them," I stated. Inside, my reaction was completely different. Calm, cool, and collected on the outside, flipping out with surprise and relief on the inside.

"I do not kill, I protect the mountain. They were held in the storm's sleep," Pamola responded mysteriously.

Does that mean he froze them? It didn't really matter, as long as they were still alive.

"You are a protector of both Man and Spirit, Wilder Black-wood. You have chosen your companions wisely. I am glad to see there are still powerful beings in the world watching over those who live." He nodded his head toward Bo, "A pity there aren't more like you. You held your considerable power in check, and that is a great strength in itself."

Bo nodded his head back at Pamola in acknowledgement, silent for once. Thankfully.

Pamola spread his wings against the backdrop of the sky, now blue and filled with puffy clouds, the last remnants of the storm having vanished along with the Kiwakwa. "They will sleep again," Pamola said. With a rumble of thunder, he melted from sight.

Bo let out a long huff, shaking frost from his jowls. "We save boy scouts, stop giants, rescue hikers, impress a god. All we get is a head nod? A thank-you pizza wouldn't kill anyone."

I laughed, even as my legs threatened to give out beneath me.

Bo reiterated. "I'm serious. Pizza."

CHAPTER TWENTY-FOUR

CLEANING UP

I t didn't take a genius to realize we couldn't just send every-one home the way they were. Boy Scouts telling stories of witnessing a battle that couldn't possibly have been real, missing hikers who were captured and then returned by an ancient mountain spirit, and oh yeah ... a freaking dragon.

Red was the first to suggest the spell to make everyone for-get. It had worked after the river battle against Draco Marinus, so it'll work this time. The spell washed over them like a gust of warm air. A couple of the kids staggered, blinking in confusion, then went right back to complaining about cold fingers and trail mix. None of them will have any recollection of what they saw, only that they were lost on a mountain in Maine and our group rescued them. The Scouts got a group rescue story, the lost hikers each got their own wilderness-survival epic. People's minds are good at filling in gaps. Plant a few details and they do the rest. They all had good stories of foraging and building shelters.

As one final precaution, I zapped the area to kill any electronics. I couldn't be too sure that one of the boys hadn't taken a photo of us. There's no cell service anywhere near the mountain, so I was certain no sneaky social media posts slipped out. No way was I going to let a blurry dragon photo leak online.

We conferred for a brief moment. "There's no cell service here to make a rescue call, and I may have accidentally fried my phone anyway. We'll fly back to town since that'll only take a few minutes. I'll make the call from the payphone at the general store."

John Patrick looked at me with a twinkle of admiration in his eyes. "Ay, laddie. I must say that was good work you did back there. You honored the mountain today. Protecting all, friend and foe alike, that's no small thing."

"I'm not sure there were any bad guys today," I answered after a moment. "Just everyone doing what they thought was right. Except for the ice demon tree people."

The Protectors took the truck and headed for home while Bo and I flew into town. I placed a call to the park rangers to let them know the missing hikers and scouts were in the parking lot. They had a lot of questions, but I just hung up the phone. All of the people we saved would only have fuzzy memories of me, Red, and John Patrick, and none at all of Bo. It seemed safer that way.

"Pizza now?" Bo asked.

"Let's get back home first. Then I'll take you to an all-you-can-eat pizza buffet."

Bo snorted. "Challenge accepted."

I already felt bad for the pizza place's kitchen staff. They had no idea what kind of storm was about to hit them.

Bo stretched and yawned, "Crisis averted. Cue the end credits."

I rolled my eyes. "Still not a catchphrase."

Bo grinned. "Give it time."

CHAPTER TWENTY-FIVE

LAUNDRY NIGHT

The twenty-four-hour laundromat at one in the morning is about the loneliest place on earth. Fluorescent lights hum like a barrel full of angry flies. The chairs are molded orange plastic, built for discomfort, and the whole place smells like detergent that probably comes in a fifty-gallon drum marked "Industrial Use Only."

I dropped into one of those Halloween nightmare chairs and watched my shirts spin in circles. Not just shirts, but the good flannel, the one without the tear in the sleeve. A sweater that didn't look like I'd fought a bear in it. A pair of jeans that could pass for respectable. Valerie deserved better than mud-stained boots and pine needles sticking out of my collar. If I was going to take her out, I needed clothes that didn't look like I lived in the woods.

Bo flopped down at my feet with the patience of someone who has lived for centuries and still thinks dinner should be served every two hours. He gave a low groan that rumbled in his chest and across the floor into my feet.

"You just ate," I said.

He snorted, eyes half-lidded, "That was hours ago."

"You had half a burger."

"Half isn't even a snack. Half is an insult."

I leaned back in the extremely uncomfortable chair and rubbed my eyes, wishing the circulation would return to my butt cheeks.

"You sound like a toddler who missed snack time."

Bo let out a yawn, opening his mouth so wide I could see every single tooth. Beneath that squashed French bulldog face lives a mighty dragon who once fought knights and hoarded gold. Now he covets snacks and long naps.

I checked the timer on the dryer. Fifteen long minutes left. The laundromat door opened, letting in a blast of cool night air. The man who stumbled in must have been searching for another bar for a nightcap, because he definitely didn't need a laundromat. He wasn't carrying any clothes to wash. The clothes he was wearing certainly needed laundering, I had to admit. He smelled like cheap whiskey and closing time.

He staggered over to a nearby row of machines, plopped down into a torture chair like it was a recliner fit for a king, and nodded off to sleep within seconds of his head leaning against the machine next to him.

Perfect. A witness.

The last thing I needed was for someone to notice anything unusual. Still, I wasn't about to change my routine. The reason I come here at one in the morning is because there's never anyone else around.

The buzzer went off on time, and I looked at the machine. Willing a bit of intent into it, the door opened, and my clothes began to parade out as if they were on a clothesline. Socks, underwear, shirts, jeans. They all drifted out, one by one, and folded in the air. All of the clothes snapped into position with precise folds, stacking themselves in the plastic chair next to me. The towels settled into a perfectly folded pile, and my jeans looked as if they were still folded on the shelf at the store. Even the socks, usually rebellious, paired up and dropped into the laundry basket.

Bo's stomach growled, making him look up at me and grumble, "If you can fold laundry without touching it, you have two free hands to make me a sandwich."

"Not happening," I laughed.

Hearing my laugh, the drunk decided to wake up briefly, sitting up and rubbing his eyes.

Blinking hard at the laundry folding itself, he admitted, "That's something new."

One sock decided to break formation at that moment and rose up into the air, zooming around the ceiling fan like a moon circling a planet. A rogue pair of boxer shorts joined the planetary garment display and whipped around the room, flapping proudly like a bird before dropping into the laundry basket.

The wide-eyed man laughed and only said one word before standing up to leave.

"Nope."

He pushed open the door and staggered out into the night, the door sliding closed behind him.

I laughed, "See, no problem. Nobody believes a drunk, not even a drunk."

I gathered my stack of folded clothes and put them all in my laundry basket.

"Finally done," Bo said.

"Nothing is open, I know what you're thinking. No sandwich. We're going home."

He stared up at me, eyes bright and ancient, the kind of look that reminded me he used to be a predator kings feared. Now he was a bulldog with food issues.

Bo climbed to his feet and shook himself, nails clicking on the tile. He padded toward the door, glanced back, and snorted once more.

"Fine. But I'm still hungry. Maybe I'll see a cat on our way back to the apartment."

I followed, basket under my arm, the laundromat flourescent flies buzzing loudly behind us. The night outside was chilly, quiet, and empty. We walked into the dark, me carrying clean clothes and him carrying the unrelenting complaint of hunger.

CHAPTER TWENTY-SIX

DON'T SHUT ME OUT

The ocean waves whispered to us as we sat on the bench, a hundred feet of sand between us and the water. Valerie met me at the restaurant after my shift, and we went down to the beach to watch the moonrise over the ocean. There were still a few autumn tourists wandering around, but mostly it was locals headed for a bar or a late-night slice of pizza and some famous Old Orchard Beach pier fries.

The air was cold enough for a light jacket or sweatshirt, just chilly enough to keep Valerie tucked in at my side for warmth. The sky was so clear that every star seemed to be carved into the inky blackness.

Bo sprawled out on the beach in front of us, letting the sand dissipate some of the furnace heat he radiated as a dragon masquerading as a bulldog. Valerie leaned against my shoulder, letting her fingers thread into mine wordlessly. I hadn't realized how much I wanted that grounding tether until she provided it.

Neither of us spoke for a long time. It was low tide, and the waves rode in and out, reflecting the silver streaks of moonlight that fell on them. The bells and electronic sounds of the nearby arcade by the pier hummed in the background, but mostly our ears were filled with the sound of the ocean. I welcomed the tranquility after the recent chaos, but it was heavy.

I closed my eyes and remembered the Kiwakwa pounding against the avalanche wall, their furl and howls echoing across the canyon. I thought of Pamola's eyes boring into mine as if he could see through to my very soul. And maybe he could. I thought of the Scouts and their faces fading into blank confusion after the memory spell. They went home with memories of getting lost in a freak storm and being rescued by strangers.

They would never know or remember how close they came to becoming another lost hiker statistic on the mountain.

My pants buzzed quietly. Only a few people have my number, so even though I was on a date, I pulled the new phone from my pocket to read the text message. It was from my grandma.

Just one line, glowing in the dark.

"Your grandfather believed the hardest battles were the ones no one ever sees."

Simple and to the point. Grandma always had a way of knowing. I let the truth of her text sink in like a stone sinking in the ocean. She didn't know what had happened on the mountain because I hadn't talked to her about it yet. The old woman had a special way of cutting right down to the bone, whether she meant to or not.

Valerie squeezed my hand. I hadn't realized how long I had been silent until she spoke. Her voice was calm and steady against the night. Warmth in the coolness.

"I don't know everything you're carrying, Wilder. But I can see it. It's there, every time you go quiet. Every time your eyes are somewhere else. Whatever it is, just don't shut me out."

I started to speak, then closed my mouth. My first instinct was always to respond with sarcasm, keeping real feelings buried. I focused on Valerie's hand in mine, the warmth of her body pressed against my side, and how good that made me feel.

"I grew up with parents who didn't really like to talk about feelings and stuff. I spent a long time not letting people in. I'm not sure where to start."

Valerie smiled and tightened her grip on my hand.

"Start small," she said, leaving a door open for the future.

Bo snorted and rolled onto his back in the sand.

"Start with me," his voice rumbled in my head. "I'm small. Compact. Easy to trust."

"Easy to trust," I repeated out loud.

She studied me for a second, then smiled. "Then maybe you're already letting me in."

Balance, I thought, isn't about slaying monsters. It's about walking the line with one foot in the human world, one in the magical, and not letting either swallow me whole. Maybe it's also about letting other people walk it with you. I smiled, squeezing Valerie's hand tighter. Whatever came next, I wasn't walking the path alone.

I looked up at the night sky where the stars hung sharp and close, like someone had cut holes in the night just to let the light through. Despite the clear weather, somewhere far off in the distance a single low roll of thunder drifted across the sky. Not a threat. Not a warning. Just a reminder.

The next wave rose out of the ocean ten feet taller than it should have been, washing all the way up to where we were sitting. The roar of water rushing over sand jolted us, and we all stepped back before the water touched our toes. Foam swirled around the bench we had been sitting on, a good hundred feet from the water's edge. Saltwater dripped from the wood as the wave hissed back toward the sea.

"That doesn't happen," Valerie said, laughing and shaking her head. "The tide doesn't just ... lunge at you."

Another wave, then a third, flooded the beach that should have been clear and dry at low tide. After the last receded, the ocean settled back to normal, but people had already gathered on the sand to investigate. A few waded in up to their ankles, pointing and murmuring, their nervous laughter carrying on the breeze as if daring the sea to explain itself.

I thought balance had been restored. I thought the mountain was enough. But the ocean had other plans.

Bo lifted his head to look at me, not joking for once about donuts or pizza. His eyes, now flashing golden with vertical slits, scanned the horizon.

"The sea is awakening," his voice said, quiet and uneasy in my head. "The gate is open."

"The world is full of magic things, patiently
waiting for our senses to grow sharper."

W. B. Yeats

AFTERWORD

Thank you for reading!

If you enjoyed this adventure, please consider leaving an honest review on Amazon or Goodreads—it helps more readers discover Wilder and Bo.

I hope you had fun exploring this book in *The Wilder Chronicles*. If you'd like to know when the next book arrives and get a few behind-the-scenes glimpses into Wilder and Bo's world, join my readers' list at the link below.

I only send updates when there's real news to share, plus the occasional story that hasn't made it into print.

-Jon

Follow the magic at http://www.jonshannonbooks.com

ACKNOWLEDGEMENTS

Love and thanks to my wife, Lori, for the encouragement.

A massive thanks to AnnaMaria, an incredible editor who saved me from numerous errors and continuity issues.

This book would not exist without the love and encouragement of my family and friends, who kept believing in me even when they were tired of hearing me talk about my stories.

Thanks to Donn Fendler's book, Lost On A Mountain In Maine, for some Chapter 14 inspiration that became central to this novel. It's remarkable true story worth reading.

Thank you to everyone who simply asked, "How's the book coming?" You have no idea how much that kept me going.

To the readers who take a chance on a Maine wizard and his dragon disguised as a dog: thank you for letting this story live in your imagination.

To everyone at WPOR and my radio family. You've taught me how to tell a story that connects.

And to Bocephus, my favorite dragon in disguise. You still owe me for the donuts.

ABOUT THE AUTHOR

Jon Shannon is a Maine author and storyteller, and a Hall of Fame broadcaster with decades of experience connecting with audiences on the radio. His fiction blends the human heart with the unseen world, exploring the magic and mystery hidden in ordinary lives.

He is the author of *The Longest Summer* and creator of *The Wilder Chronicles*, an ongoing series rooted in Maine's folklore and modern imagination.

Jon and his wife, Lori, make their home in southern Maine, where they raised their sons, Zach and Spencer, who still inspire his stories.

www.ingramcontent.com/pod-product-compliance
Lightning Source LLC
Chambersburg PA
CBHW032237310726

48973CB00008B/2180